# WHO'S THE FAIREST OF THEM ALL?

# WHO'S THE FAIREST OF THEM ALL?

•

Lynda Stowe Landers

*AVALON BOOKS*
THOMAS BOUREGY AND COMPANY, INC.
401 LAFAYETTE STREET
NEW YORK, NEW YORK 10003

Library of Congress Catalog Card Number: 98-96336
ISBN 0-8034-9316-9


PRINTED IN THE UNITED STATES OF AMERICA
ON ACID-FREE PAPER
BY HADDON CRAFTSMEN, BLOOMSBURG, PENNSYLVANIA

To Ken, my forever friend; my Big Sis; and last but not least, to the real Mary Snodgrass, who is the fairest of them all.

## *Chapter One*

Lying on her back in the baking sun, her eyes shut behind opaque sunglasses, Shay Benton listened to the glorious sound of crashing waves. She sniffed the unique, wonderful scent of salt and sea life that filled the air. She had been on this same stretch of scalloped rocky beach most of the afternoon, but when you're raised in the Texas panhandle, she thought, you can't ever get enough of the sea.

Wrapped in a world of absolute peace and quiet, Shay hoped it was going to be like this every day for the next three weeks. The first four days had been everything J. T. had promised, and more. "If God made one place in the world for R and R, it's Kolpos," J. T. had advised. Shay's destination of choice had been the mountains of Delphi. Kolpos, on the Gulf of Corinth, had received just a sentence in one of the guidebooks, no mention at all in another. But J. T. had highly recommended a pension in Kolpos, discovered on his honeymoon, over Delphi's tour buses, tavernas, and souvenir stores.

As usual, her favorite collaborator, co-vocalist, and business manager knew what he was talking about.

Kolpos was small and cheerful, popular with Greeks on holiday, relatively unknown to the outside world. And since afternoon rest periods were observed by nearly everyone, Shay had the beach pretty much to herself between the hours of one and four.

For added privacy, she had discovered this marvelous cove encircled by rocks at the edge of a lovingly protected pine forest that was a half-hour walk from the Pension Galaxidi. Not that she was likely to be recognized here, anyway.

She was already starting to tan to a rich golden brown, which contrasted nicely with her white bikini, and she had never felt so rested and relaxed in her life. She needed this break. Desperately.

At the age of twenty-four, Shay was in midstride of her biggest-selling album to date, and the past several months had brought her two Grammys, BMI's Songwriter of the Year award, a pair of back-to-back hit singles and videos, touring success, and several commercials.

Yet the whirlwind she found herself in was not entirely pleasurable.

There were no fans like those who loved country music. They were as loyal as pets, and demanded the same amount of attention. Shay sometimes felt a little like a zoo animal, tolerating the constant scrutiny of the public when they mobbed her in hotel lobbies, followed her into restaurants—for the chance to interrupt Shay Benton, with a mouthful of food, for an autograph—or drove by her home at all hours taking pictures, some actually digging up pieces of her lawn.

Shay wasn't seriously complaining, really. Nobody would ever hear her complain about her success. Success was fun! But promotional hopscotching was grueling and disorienting, especially at their current pace.

Shay and her band had just wrapped up a 270-day touring schedule, crisscrossing the United States. Christmas in Branson, Missouri . . . or was it Eunice, Louisiana? Who knew where they'd been for Thanksgiving, Easter, or Memorial Day weekend?

Holidays were for normal people, and *normal* was not a word attached to anyone who sang for their supper.

Next up—the week after she returned from vacation, to be precise—was a worldwide tour in support of the CD due out later in the summer.

The past days of sleeping late, swimming, and long walks along the beach had rejuvenated Shay. No makeup. Simple towel drying for her hair. She had yet to unpack her curling iron and hair dryer. She liked the end results, for a change.

Instead of ringlets cascading down her shoulders and spilling across her back, her mahogany-rich hair, now taking on golden highlights under the influence of the sun, flowed down her back like a piece of silk. She thought it made her look exotic, or at least as exotic as an oil-patch brat could get.

The sound of nearby voices was too soft to contend with the lulling crash of the waves. They scarcely intruded on Shay's thoughts.

"Bet you can't throw it this far."

Shay lazily turned her head to half open her eyes. Through her outsize sunglasses she glimpsed a brown blur.

The next thing she knew, a missle had dropped out of the azure sky and landed directly on her well-oiled midsection.

Her yelp came from being startled more than hurt. A boy in cutoffs and a red tank top was scrambling over the rocks. Shay sat up quickly, held the missle—a football, as it turned out—aloft. "Is this what you're looking for?"

The boy's expression registered a mixture of embarrassment and surprise. "Afraid so, ma'am," he said as he reached for the football. "Sorry 'bout that. You're not hurt, are you? Gosh, we didn't know anybody else was around here. I was running a down and in, but my brother threw a down and out."

Shay pulled her sunglasses down on her nose to stare at him. "I have no idea what language you're speaking, but I'm almost positive it's not Greek, and you don't look much like you're from around here." He was about twelve, Shay guessed, and could have been a poster boy for the all-American kid. He had sandy blond hair and a smattering of freckles across his nose, and mischievous blue eyes touched with endearing innocence. His dimpled smile was designed to break hearts, even at his tender age.

He laughed. "Heck, no, ma'am. I'm not Greek. I'm from Texas, and I guess you don't know much about football. I was talking about pass patterns. I'm on the junior-high varsity back home. I'm a wide receiver, like my brother. He's with the Houston Drillers."

Shay swallowed, with difficulty.

*The Houston Drillers?*

She wasn't sure she was still breathing.

*Sonny?*

*Don't be ridiculous,* she silently chided herself. *Such wild coincidences as that don't happen in the real world.*

Besides, even she, with her limited knowledge of football, was aware that professional teams carried more than one receiver on their roster.

*More than one from Texas?* her other side chimed.

*Texas,* she firmly reminded herself, *is a great big state. A place where football is king, from Little League through school and professional ranks.* Logic therefore dictated that in such a setting hundreds of little boys grew up to be professional athletes. Many of them receivers, no doubt, which meant that it was possible—probable, even—that more than one native son had ended up with the Drillers.

Wasn't it?

"There you are, Buddy." A man, owner of a bass voice, was standing on the rocks. He was against the sun, a silhouette. Then he was walking toward them, and Shay's eyes opened wide.

She heard the boy say, "Great aim, Sonny. You hit this pretty lady with that last pass of yours."

It was all academic by then.

It was Sonny Garrett.

Couldn't be, but it was.

Wearing swim trunks and a T-shirt embossed with the Drillers emblem, and presenting a clean-cut, healthy, athletic image, he stood between her and the sea, considering Shay with that dimpled, lopsided grin she remembered well.

Along with all the associated pain.

He had a boyish look that easily embraced all ages from sixteen to sixty. His lithe body was tanned darker than her own, a symphony of lean muscle. He had been put together with care—the sandy hair, the blue eyes, the athletic body—and exactness. He was perfection, like a sunset, a rainbow, something God had made just right.

It was too late to run, and there was no place to hide.

"I really am sorry, ma'am," Sonny said. "We didn't mean to disturb your sleep." He sounded almost too polite to be believed.

All part of the Sonny Garrett charm.

But Shay knew, better than most, the deception behind that innocent appeal.

*Slime in swim trunks,* she thought.

She found words with an effort. "I wasn't asleep."

His gaze swept over her appreciatively, with no sign that he had ever set eyes on her before. In a sense, he hadn't.

He swung his wide shoulders to glance around her little cove. "Nice place you have here."

Shay realized her teeth were clenched together. She'd never clenched her teeth before.

Her voice was frozen.

"You are American?" he asked, turning those deceptively innocent eyes back to her with a quizzical look.

The direct question forced an answer out of her. "Yes, I'm an American."

He laughed, a pleasant, husky sound. "I thought so, but I figured it was best to ask. You could be Greek, you know, with that tan. It's the eyes that threw me. They're violet, aren't they?"

"Yes."

"Are you at the Galaxidi?"

"Yes." Shay's mouth felt as if it were full of cotton balls.

Sonny gave her a long, considering look. "Are we bothering you, ma'am?"

Shay shook her head, her hand still holding the sunglasses on the end of her nose.

Sonny didn't look convinced. And, evidently feeling a touch of frostbite in the hot air, together he and his brother wandered away from Shay.

He had stared her straight in the eyes, and hadn't known!

"Of course he didn't recognize you, dummy," Shay said in an airless whisper. Why on earth would he, unless it was as Shay Benton? She still sometimes felt a sense of disconnectedness from her past self. Definitely better, this new-size body, yet occasionally the mirror reflection seemed strange and unfamiliar.

Shay slipped her sunglasses up her nose again and wrapped her arms around her knees. She sat in a kind of hypnotic trance, watching Sonny and his brother toss the football back and forth between them on the beach, as if the slightest movement would break the spell and make him vanish.

He didn't vanish.

To think that she should have met Sonny Garrett again, and in this way!

Her karma must be just to the left of the wacko zone!

Actually, the situation would have been hilarious, if it wasn't just so weird.

If it were happening to somebody else.

Come to think of it, this *was* happening to someone else, in a way. Shay Benton was vacationing in Kolpos. It was Mary Jane Snodgrass's heart Sonny had broken.

The fly in that particular ointment was that Shay and Mary Jane shared the same heart.

"What a nincompoop you were, Mary Jane." The name came out almost as blasphemy.

Sonny sprinted ahead of his brother, running a down and in—or a down and out—whatever. Time had not diminished the appeal of that clean-cut face, the engaging, big-kid demeanor that had enthralled the entire student body at Stephen F. Austin High School.

"Poetry in motion" was how the *Cap Rock Gazette* had once described his burst of speed and leaping catches on a football field.

*As graceful as a deer, as explosive as a lightning bolt. A showpiece.*

Funny how she could recall that newspaper article, practically verbatim, and yet couldn't remember where she'd spent this past Christmas.

Buddy's pass found its mark, and the brothers celebrated with a series of high fives, as if that catch had clinched a Super Bowl victory. Shay followed them with eyes that were starting to mist behind the sunglasses.

*And you deserve everything bad that can happen to you if you cry now!*

Shay shut her eyes and began to think of different ways she could torture Sonny for taking away her self-esteem and replacing it with disillusionment.

But the ghosts were gathering.

Time hitched, spun, knocked out of rhythm, the little cove full of phantoms. Shay felt as if she had stepped into some grinding nightmare where time ran backward.

Then, with an intensity she hadn't experienced before, the past came back to her.

Shay Benton disappeared and the air was full of voices. . . .

"You'll have to tutor him."

"Me?" It was an incredulous gasp.

The speaker was Stephen F. Austin's football coach. He was speaking to Mary Jane, who had come to Cap Rock, Texas, via a dozen other indistinguishable small, dusty panhandle towns. The Snodgrasses never owned a home; they moved wherever the oil was pumping. They called no place home. Stephen F. Austin High School was the ninth—or maybe it was the tenth, eleventh or twelfth—school Mary Jane had attended. She had lost track. Yet despite the constant moves, her grades never suffered. She excelled in school, especially in math courses.

Which brought her in contact with Sonny Garrett for the first time.

Sonny was a gifted athlete in three sports, excelling on the gridiron. Tall and shaggily blond, he was almost insolently beautiful. But he was a lackadaisical student in the classroom, and he was in danger of flunking geometry, which, by the no pass, no play rule, would make him ineligible for postseason play.

And as it was explained to Mary Jane by Coach Johnson, if Sonny didn't play, Austin could kiss the state championship good-bye. Sonny was the star player who had led his teammates to two divisional championships. Mary Jane was the brightest pupil in geometry class, and it was up to her to see that there was a third state championship trophy. A sacred obligation.

That was how it began.

Shay's eyes, which had lost their focus, now flicked to the tall, shaggily blond, almost insolently beautiful figure of Sonny Garrett tackling his brother no more than twenty yards away from her.

*How do I hate thee? Let me count the ways!*

Shay hoped Elizabeth Barrett Browning would forgive the paraphrasing of her beautiful poem.

*Poetry in motion.*

Shay conjured up a delicious picture of Mr. Poetry-in-motion stretched out on the sand, his limbs tied to four stakes beneath the white-hot Mediterranean sun, his tanned body covered from head to toe with honey, a swarm of killer bees, infected with rabies, swooping down on him en masse.

Samantha, the playful wife/witch from the old ''Bewitched'' television series, could accomplish that feat with a simple twitch of her cute little nose. Jeannie, the genie in ''I Dream of Jeannie,'' would cross her arms and blink.

Shay sighed longingly.

Memories flooded her mind, unbidden.

Life had picked them up and swept them along, but Shay had not lost sight of Sonny in the years since Cap Rock. Nobody had lost sight of Sonny Garrett, whose story read like something out of sports fiction: he'd gone from high school All-State to collegiate All-American; recipient of the prestigious Heisman Trophy Award, twice; number one draft pick of the Drillers; starter midway through his first season; MVP of a Super Bowl in his third season.

Sonny's name had been emblazoned on the newspapers almost every day, in every town, city, hamlet and state Shay was in, it seemed. A household name throughout the country, and, quite simply, a god in football-mad Texas.

Destined for greatness, the young man from Cap Rock, stamped ''most likely to succeed,'' had. In spades. A lovable country boy adopted by the big city . . .

* * *

"I can't tell you how much I appreciate your helping me with this darn geometry stuff, Mary Jane."

Those were the first words Sonny had said to her directly.

Mr. Butter-wouldn't-melt-in-his-mouth Garrett had been kind in other ways, too. He had taken her out for pizza, and to the Burger Boy; he had a way of making her feel special, as if she were the most important thing in his life.

*Yeah, right.*

She weighed 220 pounds, had washed-out, mousy brown hair that refused to curl, wore thick glasses, and was an Honor Society geek.

High IQ, and stupid!

She had nurtured the crazy delusion that it was her, not Tammy Sue Brenneman, who Sonny was really interested in. That it was his wish that they be together every day. That it was because he liked her that he took her out for pizza and burgers. That he could look beneath the surface of the exterior image and see the person inside.

A babe in the woods of male trees, with zilch experience in matters of the heart, she'd been dazzled, mesmerized by that football hunk; Sonny had impacted her emotions and bowled her over.

The delusion was easy to feed. They both loved country music and old movies. They had the same views on so many things—they had so much in common! They often found themselves helpless with laughter over the silliest things.

Sonny was, in fact, flatteringly attentive. He was so apparently interested in her, her views and vagabond lifestyle, that her head had been utterly turned.

He said she was easy to talk to, fun to be with.

*You know, Mary Jane, you're okay.*

Oh, the fluttering heart, the shallow breaths, the mad dreams!

The effect was intoxicating.

Shay's fingers all at once clenched into fists, her nails digging into her palms as if to punish herself for her incredible naïveté.

Had she honestly imagined that someone like Sonny Garrett could be seriously interested in someone like Mary Jane Snodgrass?

Yes. She had.

It was the first flashing, blinding, bleeding stab of love for her.

She had been like a convert to some New Age religious cult, embracing the passion without thought or logic. A teenager dreaming—and living—the impossible dream.

Temporarily, at least.

Until that memorable afternoon of her disillusionment.

Shay forced herself to conjure up the misery all over again.

Taking a break from a long geometry cramming session, she and Sonny had walked over from her house to The Donut Shop, where Mary Jane worked part-time after school and on weekends. The Donut Shop was the hangout of choice for Austin High's "in" crowd, Sonny's exclusive clique. Nerds need not apply.

Sonny joined his friends, while Mary Jane went back to the kitchen to check her work schedule for the upcoming week. Her boss, Mr. Akers, wanted to know if she could work the early weekend shift. She was more than happy to oblige.

She was almost positive that Sonny was going to ask her to be his date for the homecoming dance, and she needed a new dress. She already had one picked out at Brenneman's department store—a blue dress with sequins, surprisingly stylish, for the plus-size department. The extra pay would just about cover the cost.

After ten minutes or so, she had returned to the small eating area, six booths fronting the main counter, behind which a variety of fresh-baked donuts were displayed in glass cases. Everyone was too busy talking about the upcoming game and dance to notice Mary Jane Snodgrass.

That was why she caught every word of the conversation going on at booth number three.

It was burned indelibly into her memory banks.

"Oh, come on, Tammy Sue," Sonny was saying, his voice somewhere between frustration and amusement. "You're not serious. You can't be jealous of Mary Jane. She's a good kid and all, but you don't really think I'd be interested in someone like her."

Tammy Sue, a cheerleader with a Barbie doll's exact proportions and hair, mulled that over for a moment. Then she shrugged and said, "Well, I know it sounds silly, Sonny, but you *are* with her all the time, and I don't like it one bit!"

"For crying out loud, Tammy Sue. I don't have much choice, now, do I? Mary Jane's got all the appeal of a beached whale, but I need her to pass geometry, and you know that."

"You don't have to take her out where people can see you together. Everybody's talking, Sonny."

"It's called charity, Tammy Sue. I'll bet dollars to doughnuts that poor kid never had a date in her life, and me being the good guy that I am . . . well, I thought one good turn deserved another. You know, she's keeping me eligible for football, and I figured the least I could do was buy her a couple of burgers once in a while."

With that, Sonny laughed his trademark laugh, an infectious guffaw of such magnitude that everyone within fifty feet was forced to smile.

"I may have to ask my dad for a raise in my allowance, though, if this goes on much longer," Sonny said. "I thought I could pack away the food, but Mary Jane has me beat by a country mile. She could eat the entire football team under the table any day of the week, with one hand tied behind her back!

"The other day she devoured an entire pizza all by herself. And I'm talking large super supreme, with a side order of bread sticks. Beats me how she had room left for dessert. She managed to polish off a double-dip ice-cream cone. Ate it like she was double-parked. And she always gets food stuck between her front teeth, and then I have to look at it."

Tammy Sue said that was gross. Sonny informed her that she didn't know the half of it. Then he added, "You'd think her mother would clue her in, wouldn't you? Surely she can see what a fat slob her daughter is, even if Mary Jane hasn't looked in a mirror lately."

"Maybe a girdle would help," Tammy Sue said, giggling.

"I don't think they make whale girdles," Sonny said.

"Come to think of it," Tammy Sue said, "she does look a little like that whale we saw last summer at Sea World, doesn't she?"

"Or maybe Miss Piggy." Sonny's laughter was soft and mocking.

The object of their scorn had frozen where she stood, behind the counter and in front of the rows of sickly-sweet-smelling donuts that had helped her climb her way to 220 pounds.

She just stood there, like a beached whale, tears running down her cheeks, blubbering in her misery.

Eating a jelly-filled donut.

"And those glasses," Sonny said. "I swear, Tammy Sue, the bottoms of Coke bottles aren't that thick. It's like watching a bullfrog blinking through a fifty-pound block of ice."

"Well, I still say you're being too nice to her," Tammy Sue informed him through an exaggerated pout. "She's in love with you, you know. Anybody with half a brain and one eye can see that. Honestly, the girl is the laughingstock of the entire school, especially in gym class, and she doesn't even know it."

"Yeah, well, maybe I have been a little too charitable." Sonny's laughter, loud and cruel, drifted back to where Mary Jane stood like a statue.

She didn't hang around to hear the end of the conversation.

Somehow she willed her paralyzed limbs to move her back to the kitchen, leaving behind all the fantasy and illusion.

To this day Shay could not find adequate words to describe how she felt that day.

Heartbroken.

Humiliated.

Angry.

Hurt.

Numb.

All applicable. None accurately summed up the glowing embers of pain.

It was something she knew she would never forget.

To be forced to see herself as others saw her wasn't

a pleasant thing. Yet Sonny hadn't needed to be so cruel. If she could have confronted him there and then, thrown it all back in his face, she would have done it.

But the awful truth was that everything he said about her was true.

She had been in love with him. She was a pathetic sight. She just hadn't known how much value the world placed on image. She had known she couldn't hold a candle to the likes of Tammy Sue Brenneman, but until that moment she was totally ignorant to the importance people attached to appearances.

Sonny hadn't known her at all. That was what had really hurt her. He didn't take the time to see beneath the exterior to the real person she was under the mousy hair and ugly glasses, the extra weight and horrible clothes.

He never bothered to find out that she wasn't pathetic inside, where it counted. That she wasn't some kind of a freak with a brain. To Sonny she was never Mary Jane Snodgrass at all. She had been only a physically unattractive girl whose obvious infatuation with him had been laughable. A thing to hold in contempt. A joke to share with his girlfriend.

Well, pain was valuable to a songwriter. That particular pain was Sonny Garrett's contribution to the development of Shay Benton and her career.

For that she felt a kind of bitter gratitude.

For the rest, he was somebody she would loathe for the rest of her life.

Mary Jane had come back out of the kitchen that day, after composing herself, mumbled a half-believable excuse about an errand she had forgotten she had to run for her mother, and left The Donut Shop.

She continued to tutor Sonny, but she did not go out with him again, despite repeated invitations. She did have some pride left.

Two months after the semester finally, mercifully, ended and Sonny had passed his geometry exam, the Snodgrasses moved to California, where a new oil field was being developed outside of Bakersfield. She never saw Sonny again.

Until today.

Though her anger and hurt had been too deep for words, in music she found she could express her feelings, expose her heart without having it broken, and she channeled everything through her craft.

The homecoming dance Mary Jane never went to became the Top Ten hit "No Last Dance." Her inner battle against low self-esteem was turned into "I'm Gonna Be Somebody," which hit number one. Her disillusionment inspired "The Folly of Dreams."

"It Hurts Too Much to Cry," Shay Benton's debut album, went double platinum, was named Album of the Year by the Academy of Country Music, and resulted in her being named Best New Vocalist and Best Female Vocalist. The title cut hit number one, was

Song of the Year, and earned Shay Benton an invitation to appear on the Grand Ole Opry.

The name change had been J. T.'s idea. The Shay Benton "overnight" success story had in reality taken a while. Mary Jane had spent most of her summer vacations in Virginia, where her grandfather fronted an amateur country band. She got her start with that group when its regular bass player quit. She had learned the songs just by listening to the band's weekly rehearsals, and was asked to sit in.

In college she drove the hills and studied the Appalachian banjo pickers, helping her develop a unique acoustic style. She graduated from her grandfather's group to rock 'n' roll cover bands and fiddler revues. She dropped out of school and took the Alaska Railroad to the village of Talkeetna, where she played for tips in a roadhouse that catered to mountain climbers on their way to Denali National Park. The beavers—and Mary Jane—were enormous. The tips were not.

From Alaska she moved to San Antonio, playing the noisy bars on the Saint Mary's strip for the Trinity University crowd.

No one was listening to the plus-size silhouette blurred in the cigarette smoke and dim bar light . . . except one guy in the back, all alone, with very long hair.

Singer-songwriter J. T. Pruitt had come backstage and told her that he loved the form of her music, the way she captured ordinary, everyday concerns and brought them into her songs in an artful, even poignant manner.

He had compared her to Dylan Thomas!

She and J. T. had a terrific rapport from the beginning. He was a veteran of the Los Angeles music scene, with top credentials, and very little personal success or recognition. They developed a mutually beneficial business relationship, though the chemistry between them was strictly onstage.

She valued J. T.'s opinions, and when he suggested a name change, she agreed. Shay Benton was her beloved grandfather's name reversed.

J. T. helped Shay Benton develop her style and sound. Suddenly and miraculously she dropped a hundred pounds, and her hair fell into a perfect wave. A rinse worked wonders with the color. Contact lenses replaced the thick glasses.

They assembled a band that had experienced only one personal change to date. Their big break came when a representative of NewView Records out of Nashville caught their act at a club in Dallas, liked what she saw, and gave Shay Benton and Texas Connection a contract and a huge advance.

Shay's standard press-kit bio touched on her career, and guarded her privacy.

At the end of it all, however, Shay knew she had only half conquered the hurt. It was there, inside her, overlaid with a veil that any casual word could wisk away.

"It Hurts Too Much to Cry" got the hurt out into the open, but it had not healed.

And now Sonny Garrett was walking toward her, on a sun-drenched beach in Kolpos, and he didn't have any idea who she was!

## *Chapter Two*

It was Buddy who reached her first.

''Excuse me again, ma'am,'' he said, brushing sand from his tousled hair. ''My brother said to leave you be, but I just had to find out for sure. You are Shay Benton, aren't you, ma'am?''

''I am, minus the ma'am. Please. You make me sound like somebody's old-maid aunt.''

Buddy's grin was irresistible, and demanded one in return. ''Heck, nobody in their right mind would think that, ma'am . . . oops, sorry. That just slipped out.''

''Try calling me Shay.'' She took a deep breath. Her pulse rate was just settling down to normal as Sonny approached.

He looked down at her with an apologetic smile. ''You'll have to excuse my brother's bad manners, ma'am. He was raised better. It's just that he's a huge fan of yours."

"Yeah, and so's he," Buddy countered. Then, with a superior, challenging look in his brother's direction, "Shay doesn't like being called ma'am, Sonny. It makes her feel real old."

Shay couldn't help laughing. And Sonny said, "Tact never was one of the twerp's long suits." He could not repress a crooked, embarrassed smile. "He is telling the truth, though. I . . . we're both big fans of yours, Ms. Benton. We didn't recognize you right off. Probably because your hair's different and you're wearing those sunglasses. It hit us both at the same time. But I told Buddy he shouldn't disturb you any more than we already have.

"I know what it's like to have well-intentioned fans bug you when you want privacy," he added.

"Oh? Are you someone I should know?" Shay asked impulsively.

If she had struck him Sonny could not have looked more surprised. He cleared his throat. He looked from Shay to Buddy, then back to Shay again, his expression suddenly reminding her of that of a shy schoolboy about to ask a girl out on a first date. "I'm—" He cleared his throat a second time. "I'm . . . well, the thing of it is, I'm a football player, and back in the States everybody knows this face."

Shay smiled blankly. Both she and Mary Jane were enjoying his awkwardness.

"You really don't know who I am, do you?" Sonny's stunned expression was priceless, surpassed only by his disbelieving tone of voice; together they presented a total package of someone whose ego had been stepped on, trampled on, big-time.

*His nose is too long and bony,* Shay thought. *His hair is too blond, his eyes such a pale shade of blue as to seem faded—and who wants dimples on a grown man?*

His teeth weren't perfect, either.

"No," she said. "I'm sorry." Again the lie slipped out so easily it surprised her.

"I'm Sonny Garrett." He paused, as if waiting to see if the name rang any bells. Shay's blank expression was frozen in place, behind which she barely managed to resist a very strong impulse to laugh in his face. "I'm a wide receiver for the Houston Drillers."

"I already told her that," Buddy said, rolling his eyes.

"Yes, as a matter of fact he did," Shay concurred. "And that's the problem. I'm not a fan of the game. It's much too violent for my taste."

"Oh." Sonny didn't seem to know what else to say.

Shay and Mary Jane shared an inward smile of satisfaction and self-gratification.

"Tell Shay about the time you almost met her," Buddy urged, sitting down next to Shay.

''There's nothing to tell,'' Sonny said, almost reluctantly.

''Sure there is,'' Buddy insisted, grinning from ear to ear. ''You're just too embarrassed to admit the truth.'' He turned to Shay. ''See, my brother's in love with you. He plays your CDs everywhere he goes on the road, and in the clubhouse, too. All the guys tease him about it. And he wanted to meet you in person, real bad—''

''Gee, thanks for sharing that, Buddy,'' Sonny interrupted. ''Remind me to wring your neck later.'' He offered Shay a helpless smile. ''Now that the twerp has totally humiliated me I suppose there's no way of getting around the rest of the story.'' He was so shy about it he was literally kicking the sand as he talked.

''I'd like to hear it,'' Shay invited, her interest piqued.

Sonny looked down at his feet, and then burst out laughing. ''Sure, why not? I'll give it a whirl, anyway.'' He shrugged and joined them on the sand. The warm skin of his shoulder brushed Shay's for a moment, making her flinch as though she'd been touched with a hot branding iron.

''About a year ago,'' Sonny began, ''the Drillers were in Dallas for a Sunday game against the Cowboys. You were playing at one of the local clubs. I can't recall the name of the place now, but that Saturday night a bunch of us went to see you, and after the show we waited at the stage door for over an hour. You never showed."

"He had flowers for you, and everything," Buddy said.

"Oh." Now it was Shay who couldn't think of anything else to say.

Sonny seemed to hesitate with painful shyness before he spoke again. "I know you probably hear this all the time, and I hope it doesn't sound too corny, but I can't tell you how much I enjoyed that show. You closed with a medley of your hits. Everybody in the audience loved it. Faces lit up with every song you started to play, and when you finished the roar of approval was almost deafening.

"But my favorite part was when you sat on a stool in the center of the stage, with a purple spotlight on you, and sang 'It Hurts Too Much to Cry.' That just blew me away. Oh, and in case you're interested, it was roses."

"What was roses?"

"The flowers Big Mouth was talking about." Sonny reached around behind Shay and playfully swatted Buddy on top of the head. "They were put to good use, though. They quite possibly saved a marriage, in fact. Our center had forgotten his wedding anniversary. His wife loved the roses."

Fighting an insane urge to giggle, Shay said, "I'm glad, and thank you for the kind words." She was tempted to blurt out the whole truth, then thought better of it.

What on earth would she say?

*Hey, Sonny, it's me, Mary Jane Snodgrass. Remember her? That fat, brainy nerd from Cap Rock? Well, would you look at her now. The beached whale who had such a crush on you grew up to be the woman you brought roses to. Imagine that. Oh, and by the way, Sonny, that song that just blew you away? Well, guess what, Sonny—I wrote it about you!*

*Uh-uh, no way!*

There was silence while Shay thought about things she could not put into words. "Are you staying at the Pension Galaxidi too?" she asked at last.

Sonny nodded. "We arrived yesterday."

"This is my birthday present," Buddy said. "I'll be twelve tomorrow. I promised Sonny I wouldn't cramp his style with the ladies if he brought me along. So . . ." He came slowly to his feet. "I guess it's time for me to get out of here." He grinned hugely. Shay thought she was already in love with this pint-size version of Sonny Garrett.

Hopefully, this Garrett would grow up knowing something about compassion.

"In case you haven't noticed, the twerp has a fresh mouth," Sonny said. The affection in his heart for his brother was so obvious that Shay couldn't help being touched.

Then Mary Jane nudged her hard from the past, reminding her who she was dealing with.

Shay swallowed around the lump that had gathered in her throat.

After extracting a promise from Shay that she'd send him an autographed picture, Buddy headed back to the pension. He left behind another awkward pause.

Shay cleared her throat.

Sonny nervously scratched his chin, then said, "What about you, Ms. Benton? Are you here with friends?"

"I'm on my own. And it's Shay," she added, biting back another urge to tell him who she really was.

"Greece is a long way to come on your own. If you don't mind my asking, how did you find this place? Most people have never heard of Kolpos."

"A good friend recommended it for rest and relaxation. Something I needed. What about you?"

"Same thing. My agent comes here often, usually during the winter. He said it was a place where I'd be able to swim without being recognized." He glanced at Shay with a slow, significant smile. "Seems he was right."

"I'm sorry if I bruised your ego," Shay lied.

Sonny laughed. "To tell you the truth, until now I didn't even know I had one. But I'll survive."

"Yes, I'm sure you will." The tension was too much for her; making small talk with Sonny was just too much. Shay knew that if she didn't get away now she would say or do something really stupid.

With a nervous movement, she gathered up her towel and straw bag, and rose fluidly to her feet. "It's time for me to get out of the sun."

"Sure. I understand. I didn't mean to disturb you."

"You didn't. I really am too hot."

"Maybe I'll see you at dinner." His glance was disturbingly penetrating.

"Maybe," Shay said, slightly breathless, turning away.

She walked quickly up the beach away from him. She felt his eyes dwelling on her back, and knew in her bones that he was watching the swing of her long legs.

By the time Shay got back to the pension her skin was damp with nerves. She walked the flower-lined path into the courtyard that was luxuriant with blossoms. A fountain burbled, classical music played, and the pleasingly round owner of Pension Galaxidi, Bruno Demetri, sat at a table, reading and smiling.

He greeted Shay in schoolbook-perfect but halting English and handed her a slip of paper. "You had a phone call while you were out, my dear," he said. "From the States."

"Thanks." Shay didn't have to look at the scribbled message to know who had called. J. T. was the only person who knew where she was.

The interior of the inn was simple and cheerful, unself-consciously decorated with books and religious art. Shay walked up the creaky stairs to her small room on the second floor that had a double bed, private bath, a church incense burner as a chandelier, and a breathtaking view from the window: low, cultivated hills and red-tile roofs, with a medieval wall angling across the landscape.

She wriggled out of her bikini and stepped under a cool shower.

The giggle was reflexive; it was the admiring light she'd seen in Sonny's eyes that tickled her.

Imagine Sonny Garrett flirting with the former beached whale!

If nothing else, this chance meeting with Sonny was good for a few laughs, and just a trace of redemption.

Shay giggled again as a mental image of Sonny standing at that stage door, clutching a bouquet of roses, flashed through her mind.

But she had no idea what had possessed her to carry this thing so far. She should have told him who she was the moment they met.

Some mischievous part of her was glad she hadn't.

Let him find out who she really was, if he could, and suffer the humiliating embarrassment.

It would serve him right.

The thought of seeing the look on his face if and when he did had a most pleasing tang for her. She'd certainly enjoyed his priceless expression when she pretended she had never heard of him.

*He who laughs last, laughs the loudest.*

*Or in this case,* she *who laughs last.*

Shay stepped out of the shower and dried herself. Wrapping another towel around her hair, she slipped into her terry-cloth robe and went into the other room to read the message that Bruno had given her.

It was from J. T., and it wasn't good news. On her upcoming CD she played a set of songs that ranged from keenly detailed explorations of love lost, found, or wanted, to evocations of starry nights that had given an overweight teenager hope, to a two-stepping celebration of good times, Texas style. But in planning for the recording session, J. T. had discovered they were a song short, and time was running out.

"Hate bothering you on vacation, sweetheart," the message stated. "But get it in gear as soon as possible. Fax, if you can find a machine. Like yesterday."

Shay plopped down on the edge of the bed with a weary sigh. She had a few songs, and pieces of possible songs in her files at home. "Wads of loose papers," J. T. called them. She had been so busy on the road lately that she hadn't had time to concentrate on her writing.

Then it occurred to her that once again Sonny Garrett just might be the one to provide the stimulation for her creative juices. He had unknowingly inspired "It Hurts Too Much to Cry," the song that had been a testament to Mary Jane's heartache, and vaulted her alter ego to stardom.

This time it was a chance meeting at a Greek resort

that had all the delicious earmarks of evening a few old scores. The stuff number one hits were made of.

Shay decided that "Vindication" was a good working title.

She hadn't come here to work—but this could be fun!

It was one of those things that flowed out in about fifteen minutes, retitled, "Cowgirls Don't Get Mad, They Get Even." The song plotted a hysterically funny course of seduction and revenge that topped any soap opera conspiracy ever devised.

On paper only—wasn't it?—Shay reminded herself, as she slipped on a pair of white shorts and a blue T-shirt, brushed her damp hair, and headed back downstairs.

Bruno, still reading and smiling, said that the nearest fax machine was at a hotel in Delphi, about thirty minutes away. He graciously offered Shay the use of his car, which turned out to be about the size of a car-shaped suit, and was not air-conditioned.

The site, however, was thrilling—high in the mountains with powerful views that surely helped inspire the world to believe the words from the oracle that was located there.

By the time she had faxed the lyrics to J. T., for his musical interpretation on the other end, and returned to the Pension Galaxidi, Shay was dirty, sweaty, and needed another shower. And she was beyond hungry; she was famished.

And she missed Obadiah, the Lhasa apso she'd rescued from the pound, desperately. So much that she had added a personal footnote to the fax, telling J. T. to give Obadiah a big hug and kiss from his "mommy."

He'd say he did, and wouldn't.

After her second shower, Shay dressed in a light and airy white peasant blouse and full multicolored cotton skirt that brought out the rich coloring of her hair and skin. She looped a string of taupe tortoiseshell beads round her neck, and added matching bangles for her arms. She fixed her hair in a fat, glossy braid that hung down her back, applied just a touch of lip gloss, and surveyed herself in the full-length mirror.

*This situation might be fun, after all.*

The vindictive streak Shay hadn't been aware existed in her before was beginning to rear its ugly head again.

She went down to dinner feeling as though she were going onstage for the performance of her life, plugged into the electric current along with her guitar.

Sonny and Buddy joined Shay at one of the canopy-covered tables outside the inn's small restaurant. They all ordered the same thing: moussaka, a sort of eggplant lasagna. Shay was feeling a lot more poised in Sonny's company.

And she was thoroughly enjoying being the only one in on her private joke!

Sonny asked her about singing and writing, and he wanted to know where she came from.

"I know you're a native Texan," he said. "I wouldn't be much of a fan if I didn't know that. But I've never heard exactly where in Texas you're from."

"I was born in Kilgore, but my family moved around so much that I don't really call anyplace home."

"Like in your songs," Buddy said. " 'No Place Child' and 'Where Are You Now?' "

Shay smiled at the boy. "Exactly, and thank you for remembering, Buddy. You're good for my ego."

Buddy's grin was heartrendingly sweet.

"A kind of biographical fiction," Sonny put in.

Shay ate a mouthful of moussaka before answering. "You could say that." Then she rattled off the standard press-kit bio: the "exclusive" story of the life and times of the oil-patch kid who made good, with no real specifics. Nothing that could be traced back to Mary Jane Snodgrass or Cap Rock. It came so naturally now that Shay hardly remembered her real background.

"What about 'It Hurts Too Much to Cry'?" Sonny asked.

Shay felt her heart skip a beat. She took a slow sip of her water. "What about it?"

"Well, I can't help being curious. You've admitted

that your songs are based on reality, for the most part. I was wondering if that one fit into the category."

"That's really none of your business."

"You're right. Forgive me. I didn't mean to pry into your personal life. Besides, there's not a man alive who would treat you the way that jerk acted in your song. You are beautiful," he added, his voice trailing off until it was no more than a murmur. "You . . . dazzle me."

"What a sweet thing to say," Shay said, trying not to laugh. "But if it's all the same to you, I'd just as soon change the subject."

"Why?"

"I don't like talking about myself."

"Ah, you prefer being a lady of mystery."

Shay put down her fork and propped her chin on her clasped hands. "I just don't happen to think people really need to know what I do offstage. There's nothing mysterious about that. It's called privacy."

"I can identify with that." The smile made Sonny suddenly breathtakingly handsome, and guileless. "I've had to deal with those trash stories in tabloids that intrude on your privacy and yet get all the facts wrong. That's why I avoid reporters whenever possible, and when an interview is necessary I stick to the facts. 'Just the facts, ma'am,' as Joe Friday would say."

"Don't tell me you watch 'Dragnet' reruns."

"Guilty. I've seen most of the episodes so many

times I know the dialogue by heart. Those old TV reruns are my main passion in life. I go to bed most nights with Mary.''

''Which one?''

''Take your pick. I can never decide who I love more, Mary Tyler Moore as Laura Petrie or as Mary Richards.''

''What about Bob Newhart?''

''And 'Taxi'?''

'' 'Happy Days'?''

''May I please be excused now?'' Buddy interrupted, plainly bored with their oldies-but-goodies TV review.

Sonny nodded. ''Sure, twerp, but stay out of Mr. Demetri's hair, and mind your manners.'' He watched his brother leave through a break in the bougainvilleas and hibiscus, then returned his attention to Shay with a smile. ''I think Buddy's experiencing his first case of puppy love. It's Mr. Demetri's daughter, Eugenie. Do you remember your first love?''

''Yes.'' Shay smiled, with effort. ''What about you?''

He considered the question thoughtfully. ''That would be Tammy Sue Brenneman, I suppose.''

Shay was sorry she'd asked. ''And it didn't work out?'' she asked, making her tone hearty.

Sonny shook his head. ''Naw. First loves rarely do. At that age it's probably more being in lust than in love, anyway.'' He studied her. ''I'm sure you left a trail of broken hearts as you traveled the land.'' His eyes were warm.

''Not really. I was a late bloomer.'' Shay had finished eating, and he still didn't know who she was. ''Please excuse me,'' she said, rising. ''I enjoyed the meal and the conversation.''

Sonny rose with automatic courtesy. ''Do you really have to go? It's still early, and there's a nice place over by the pier—''

Shay cut him off with a shake of her head. ''I'm sorry, but I have other plans. Maybe some other time.''

''I guess I'll see you at the beach, then,'' he said.

Shay felt his eyes boring into her back as she walked away.

She smiled, and muttered under her breath, ''Enjoy the view, Garrett.''

## *Chapter Three*

"We've got to stop meeting like this," Sonny whispered in Shay's ear as he joined her for breakfast a few mornings later. "People are beginning to talk already."

Shay fought to suppress the hysterical giggle at the thought that the boy who had once described her as a beached whale and Miss Piggy, among other things, had evolved into this man who couldn't get enough of her the past few days. More than once he had complimented her on her beauty and charm.

Such was the power of a change in appearance.

"Eating at the same table hardly constitutes cohabitation," Shay said.

Sonny flashed that toothy grin—the most famous smile in all of Texas. "Maybe not, but I know married couples who don't eat together as often as we do.''

Shay dug into her grapefruit and gave him a sidelong glance. He looked extremely attractive and outdoorsy in a white T-shirt and cutoff jeans that made the best of his muscled legs. She forced herself to keep up the light, cool tone she had adopted from their first exchange. ''I'm willing to risk it if you are.'' They'd gotten into the habit of lunching together, and had had dinner together the night before too.

Sonny offered up a helpless shrug. He said nothing, but the way he was looking at Shay made her avert her eyes and begin to fiddle with her grapefruit again.

Sonny picked up the menu. ''Did you get a good night's sleep?''

''Slept like a baby.'' Shay finally looked up at him again. ''Where's Buddy?''

''Three guesses, and the first two don't count.''

''Eugenie.''

''Give the lady a cigar. He'll be along in a few minutes. He's helping the young lady milk goats, so it must be love. That's fresh goat milk you see offered on the Galaxidi menu, incidentally, in case you were wondering.''

''I wasn't. I don't drink milk, of any kind.''

''Really? I love the stuff, especially milk shakes. This will be my first experience with the goat variety, though.'' He turned to Bruno, who had materialized beside them, and, to go with the bread, ordered chutneys and butters, served with Bruno's homemade preserves, and a glass of goat's milk for his alfresco breakfast. Shay took advantage of Bruno's presence to ask for a fresh pot of coffee.

"That is fresh coffee, Miss Shay," Bruno informed her, beaming proudly. "Fresh coffee you always get at Pension Galaxidi. Not that ubiquitous Nescafé served at the harbor cafés."

Swallows wheeled above, Italian opera wafted on the soft air, Bruno was solicitous. Somewhere in the twisting streets below, children played soccer, and the happy noise drifted up. It was dreamlike, a defining moment.

They had spent most of yesterday afternoon on the beach, talking and swimming. Sonny hadn't suspected for a moment that he knew her.

Last night, over Bruno's memorable Greek home cooking, Shay kept waiting for Sonny's memory to return, with some connection between girl past and woman present. Her chatter seemed to come out of nowhere, someone else's voice sliding past her perpetually smiling lips. She had felt as if she were sitting on pins and needles, waiting for the other shoe to drop.

Now she relaxed in the confidence that Sonny was strongly attracted to a woman he would never recognize as the Cap Rock, Texas, laughingstock. The boot was on the other foot this time, and Shay had to admit that it was a hoot being the one holding the upper hand.

She had cast the bait, and Sonny fell for it, hook, line, and sinker.

And he was making a complete fool of himself as she slowly reeled him in!

Yet Shay wasn't so blind, or full of herself, not to recognize the pattern.

History repeating itself.

Mr. Butter-wouldn't-melt-in-his-mouth Garrett, drinker of milk shakes, wasn't interested in Shay Benton the person. She was a trophy date. A body that filled out a bikini to his liking.

*Jerk.*

Appearance was all that mattered, again. Everything else was irrelevant.

It had been on the tip of her tongue several times the past few days to tell him the truth, and then relish the look on his face as realization set in. But, as it had become clearer that he still didn't have the remotest idea who she was, Shay had decided to keep her little secret a while longer, to wait and see how things would turn out.

*Give him enough rope to hang himself!*

When Sonny walked her to her room last night after dinner, Shay had seen the kiss coming, and she just let his lips touch hers, barely a graze, before she drew quickly away. Then, with a faint smile, she locked herself in her room.

Mary Jane would have given her right arm, and several other important limbs, for a kiss from Sonny Garrett.

Shay Benton was left cold by him and his superficiality, the cruelty she knew he was capable of.

*And Shay Benton is a liar, and not a very good one. You know your toes curled, just a little,* that carping voice inside her head continued, and Shay took ten deep breaths.

Buddy and the fresh pot of coffee arrived at the same time. The youngest in a family of five boys, Buddy had unofficially adopted Shay as his big sis, and he was chattering brightly as he slid into the chair next to Shay. His first goat milking experience had been "cool," said with the engaging Garrett grin.

"The goats or Eugenie?" Shay asked with a grin of her own. "Eugenie is awfully cute."

"Sure she is," Buddy said. "But you know what's really neat about her, Shay? See, she wants to be a vet, and you've never seen anybody who loves animals like Eugenie does. She's drawn to them, and they're drawn to her. The Demetris have four dogs and six or seven cats. Maybe more than that. They were running all over the place, so it was hard to count them. Anyway, Eugenie has this way with animals that is so cool. A special gentleness, I guess you'd call it, even with the goats. I've never met anyone like her before in my life. She's really a nice person, Shay."

"I'm sure she is, Buddy, and you're not half bad yourself." It was good to know that at least this

Garrett knew what to value and prize. Eugenie, the animal lover, was a girl after Shay's heart.

"Thanks," Buddy said, coloring slightly. "You're pretty neat yourself. I just know you'll like Eugenie. I asked her to go to the beach with us today. She said she would, if she gets through with her chores in time. You are coming to the beach this morning, aren't you?" he asked hopefully.

"Yep." Shay pulled back the shoulder of her cotton shirt to show the red strap of her swimsuit. "I'm ready."

"Great!" Buddy's eyes cut mischievously to Sonny. "Think we should let him come along?"

"I'll have to think about that." Shay smiled. "What do you want for breakfast?"

"A cheeseburger."

"Sorry. No cheeseburgers," Shay said regretfully, consulting the menu.

"Try the *dolmades*," Sonny suggested. "It won't make you forget the Burger Boy, but it's good with the chutney." He turned to Shay. "Burger Boy is as close as you get to a Dairy Queen in our hometown. We're from a hiccup of a place way out in West Texas, Cap Rock. I'm sure you've never heard of it. Few have. I'm not even sure it's on any map. It's not much to look at. There's not a tree in sight. But Burger Boy makes the best hamburgers you've tasted in your life."

"I don't eat red meat," Shay managed to get out,

once again experiencing the lump in her throat that now threatened to undermine her composure.

She picked up her spoon and swirled a sugar cube in her coffee, watched a rambunctious kitten tumble among the tables. Buddy said it was either Zeus or Jupiter.

"It's one of Eugenie's cats," he explained. "But it's hard to tell which one. Zeus and Jupiter are identical twins."

Butterflies waltzed to the Italian opera that continued to play softly in the background. "What is a *dolmade*?" Shay asked when she felt confident enough to speak again without sounding like a mockingbird with the croup. "I was afraid to risk ordering it."

Sonny laughed. "So was I, at first. The most exotic thing I've ever had for breakfast is an omelette. But I decided, what the heck. Nothing ventured, nothing gained. Right? And it's not bad. *Dolmades* are stuffed grape leaves. I wasn't adventuresome enough to ask what they're stuffed with."

"Sounds yucky," Buddy said. But he tried the *dolmades* anyway, and when the stuffed grape leaves arrived Shay sampled one, and both she and Buddy decided they were delicious, whatever they were stuffed with.

They lingered long over breakfast. Then as soon as Eugenie had fed all her animals and joined them, they went down to the beach.

It was another glorious morning, the sun blazing

down from a cloudless sky. They discarded their cover-up clothing and plunged into the wonderfully warm water. Shay swam until she was exhausted, then stretched out on the sand to dry.

She watched Sonny swim, his muscular shoulders cutting an easy swath through the surf. Buddy and Eugenie were clambering on limestone rocks beaten into fantastic shapes by wind and water. Eugenie was dark-haired and lovely. She had her mother Sophie's silver dollar-sized dark eyes and her father's cork-popping personality, and she had obviously taken a strong fancy to Buddy, and vice versa.

Shay welcomed their presence, subscribing to the safety-in-numbers theory. It was a relief to have the rather dangerous flirtation that had been developing between her and Sonny curtailed for a while.

Shay was finding flirting with Sonny Garrett to be a definite strain.

She wasn't that well versed on the art of coquetry, anyway, though she had read *Gone With the Wind* twice.

The beach had a quiet morning appearance. A few sun worshipers were stretched out on the sand. One health enthusiast, a man with a face that suggested middle age and a body that fit into bikini swim trunks better than most twenty-year-olds would, was jogging. Under the watchful supervision of a plump woman in a colorful sundress and wide-brimmed straw hat, two little girls were wading in the surf.

After a while, Sonny emerged, dripping, and dried himself vigorously. Shay couldn't take her eyes off him, fascinated by the way his body moved, the powerful muscles pulsing and relaxing in such perfect harmony. He was a big, leanly built man who wore his rangy body with the assurance and grace of a delicate animal—a deer.

He was magnificent, really. Stunningly good-looking, his hair curling even though he wore it short. He clearly possessed all those vague characteristics called variously magnetism, grace, distinction, attractiveness, and fascination, all going to make up the nebulous quality known as charm—and never was Sonny Garrett quite so charming as when he smiled.

No one could possibly be immune to that devilish, boyish smile that seemed to put him at odds with the sense of full-adult masculinity that emanated from him.

Shay felt aroused, exposed, and suddenly defenseless, feelings that made her want to run away from him and this situation posthaste.

*Darn it, Shay, get a grip on yourself! You're not that silly, pathetic teenager with a crush on the local football hero anymore. And you'd best be remembering that, as nice as he seems now, this man you're drooling over wouldn't give you the time of day if you were still walking around in Mary Jane's shoes.*

Sonny flopped down beside Shay on his back, closing his eyes with a sigh. "This is the life, isn't it? I don't even want to think about going back to the real world."

Shay pretended to be absorbed in the magazine she'd brought along. She was really thinking about herself. About Mary Jane Snodgrass, and about Sonny.

Especially about Sonny.

Reminding herself why she hated him.

She turned her head slightly to study Sonny. Even in repose his mouth gave out a warm and unobstructed smile. To catch sight of it unexpectedly was to feel a little better. It gave his face a wistful look, a certain vulnerability that could melt the hardest of hearts.

*Unless you'd already been there, done that, bought the T-shirt!*

As her father was fond of saying, Fool me once, shame on you. Fool me twice, shame on me.

And that all-American package wrapped up in a toothpaste-advertisement smile had had his go at shattering her heart.

*Remember, Cowgirls don't get mad, they get even!*

His broad chest moved in a slow, tranquil rhythm as Sonny dozed off in the sun. Beads of water glistened like pearls against his bronzed skin. What would it be like to reach out and touch that muscular throat, trace the way it met the bending curve of his collarbone, continue across those pectoral muscles to the washboard stomach?

The idea was both exciting and frightening.

Shay looked away, weird feelings turning her blood to ice, then to flame.

*Well, what did you expect, for crying out loud?*

She had once had a monumental crush on this jerk, and she couldn't pretend total indifference now.

No healthy female alive could feel indifferent to this man.

*So what do you feel, Shay?*

Avoiding the question, she moved her gaze to Buddy and Eugenie, who were laughing as they watched a yacht try to anchor in a nearby green cove; the yacht was doing 360s in the currents, nearly bonking a nearby yacht, forcing its owner to get up from his nap and look at the other yacht with a perturbed expression. Then Shay returned to her magazine, *Guide to Guitars Past and Present.*

Sonny turned his head lazily toward her, opening his eyes. A sturdy innocence shone from those baby-blues, and for a brief moment Shay was back in Mary Jane's shoes again—an experience that left her with the bitter taste of rotten memories.

''A drachma for your thoughts,'' Sonny said.

Shay shook sand off her magazine. ''Is that the Greek equivalent of a penny?''

''A drachma is worth about thirty cents. I'm no cheapskate.''

''I'm flattered, but you'd be wasting your money. I wasn't thinking. I'm reading.''

He rolled onto his stomach, laughing softly. ''Are you really reading that magazine?''

She wasn't, but improvised without missing a beat. ''There's a fascinating article on the 1950 Fender Broadcaster guitar. It's very rare, especially in butterscotch.''

''That's almost as fascinating as someone who can read upside down.'' He reached out and reversed the magazine. ''There,'' he said with a glint in his eyes. ''Maybe you'll be able to make heads or tails of that article now.''

Shay couldn't help laughing as she tossed the magazine aside. ''Okay, so I wasn't reading. Chet Atkins himself couldn't concentrate on guitars in this gorgeous setting.'' She didn't expound on the specific view she'd recently been enjoying.

''You're right about that,'' Sonny agreed. ''This place is something else. Pretty beaches, and more alfresco dining than a sleepy town needs. I was thinking about seeing some of the other local color. Bruno's a walking, talking historian, plus he's offered me the use of his car. Buddy's interested in seeing ruins. He likes all that ancient gods and goddesses stuff. At least he does since he met Eugenie, who's quite the expert on the subject. I thought this afternoon would be a good time to go exploring. You're welcome to come along with us. I'm assuming you can tear yourself away from that fascinating magazine.''

"Oh, gosh, I'm not sure I could do that," Shay said, and rolled her eyes theatrically.

"What if I sweeten the pot with a couple of drachmas?"

"Which is about what Bruno's car is worth. Have you actually seen it?"

"No. Why? Is something wrong with it?"

Blinking with a mind's-eye picture of her trip to Delphi, Shay said, "Let's just say you're in for an unusual experience, and leave it at that."

Sonny grinned. "I love surprises. But it couldn't be any worse than the first old clunker I had. I was seventeen. The car was about twenty-five. . . ."

Shay's own vivid recollections tumbled into Sonny's voice. It was a VW Beetle, yellow, with terminal dead batteryitis.

Never fear, Tammy Sue Brenneman and her shiny red Corvette to the rescue.

Shay found herself staring blankly at the surf as Sonny's voice droned on.

*What have I gotten myself into?*

She should have told him who she was right away.

Then, as a huge, hot hurting ballooned briefly inside her chest, Shay shook away the feelings of doubt, along with the carping voice inside her head that sent out periodic warning signals that this adventure was something she might well live to regret.

She took ten deep breaths.

*Let him stay fooled. At least for a while.*

She'd feed him some humble pie for dinner, and maybe he'd earned a nice dessert too. Such as the one she had playfully plotted in "Cowgirls Don't Get Mad, They Get Even."

The "cowgirl" was suddenly gone one morning, leaving the guy a mocking note, telling him who she really was and reminding him of how he had once found her so pathetically absurd.

She'd leave him with a couple of side dishes and condiments, humiliation and anger, as examples.

She'd leave Sonny Garrett with what the bird left on the driveway, wondering what had hit him.

Shay felt instantly calmer.

Sonny did say he loved surprises.

## *Chapter Four*

The worst possible thing happened: Shay had a good time.

Eugenie, having traveled Greece extensively with an older married sister and her family, was an excellent tour guide. They had headed out along the coastal highway that had olive and orange orchards dotting the inland side of the road, the deep blue sea stretched out on the other.

Then they found themselves in a wide, baking valley, where, now ravenous, they ate cheese pies at a scenic mountain taverna.

They ate enormously, talked prodigiously, and at different points laughed so hard that tears ran down their faces. Shay didn't think she had ever laughed with quite the same heartiness before.

And at various times she reminded herself that the object was not to have fun.

For all the good it did her.

She was going to have to work really hard on the revenge thing.

She even enjoyed being crammed into the front seat of Bruno's sweltering car-shaped suit with Sonny, Buddy, and Eugenie likewise shoulder to shoulder in the back. A double date, of sorts.

They arrived at the ancient village of Kristos during peak afternoon heat. That didn't keep them from hiking along a path that led upward to a ruined castle, scrambling over rocks between two low walls.

Where the walls had crumbled away, the path was a series of holes gouged out of the rock, forming a circular pattern around the domelike hill. Around and around it went, until there came a break that allowed ascent to another tier. Then another. And another. It was an effective and exhausting deterrent, Eugenie explained, for all but the most persistent of enemies. The mazelike path required a sharp eye and a sure foot.

By the time they reached the top they were beaten down by the heat, sun, dust, and long hike. They were dirty, sweaty, and hungry again. But they weren't running low on fun.

There it was, that dreadful *F* word again: Fun!

They crossed a sagging bridge to learn that the castle was only toppled columns and heaped rubble. "I guess that's why they're called ruins," Sonny said.

"Brilliant deduction, Garrett," Shay said, and started to laugh. Sonny joined her. Then Buddy and Eugenie were laughing too.

Though all that remained standing was a tower three stories high, the sight of it filled Shay with the sensation of having left her own time and crossed to another, much earlier one.

They climbed the tower's stone steps so they could view the countryside through the narrow windows in its side. Eugenie said that Hercules supposedly buried the giants somewhere in the area. As Sonny helped Shay up a difficult spot, his strong hands touched her body with a possessive appreciation that set her blood racing.

*Serves you right,* her carping voice continued.

Shay took ten deep breaths.

Next, Eugenie took them on a tour of the old village, where they munched gyros and were watched over by a white church that glowed in the magic light of late afternoon. The flagstone streets around the harbor and the narrow cobblestone walking streets, called *thromakis*, according to Eugenie, were draped with bougainvillea and lined with traditional Mediterranean facades.

By the time they got back to Kolpos they were happily exhausted. As they piled out of the car, Buddy declared it the coolest day of his life. "Heck, this was even better than the time Sonny took me to the Alabama Coushatta Indian Reservation," he added earnestly. His eyes never left pretty Eugenie, whose face was adorably flushed beet red.

Sonny said, "On a scale of one to ten, I'd have to rate today at least a twenty." His eyes were directly on Shay as he spoke. His dazzling smile, bracketed by those dimples, made it unthinkable not to smile back. It certainly had been one of Shay's better days.

Her quality-control alarm went off.

*This is a dangerous game you're playing,* her carping voice resumed.

Sonny invited her to spend the next day with them.

Shay said yes.

Later, alone in her room, she reminded her irritating carping voice that it was all part of the plan.

Granted, there were certain perils involved. But the rewards in this case were going to be very sweet.

*Cowgirls don't get mad, they get even.*

She just had to be careful that she didn't keep getting her britches caught on her own pitchfork.

As she stepped out of the shower, Shay turned to the full-length bathroom mirror and studied her reflection dispassionately. Her mind drifted back to a time when she had looked in other mirrors, and almost made out a thinner version of Mary Jane Snodgrass, just aching for company, but it had been held inmate in a fat holding cell.

There wasn't a trace of excess fat on Shay Benton's tall, slim frame. Her breasts were a bit too big, but that never did a girl any harm. Her legs were remarkably long and remarkably shapely; she could say that without vanity.

Sonny was interested in her; she could say that without vanity too, and knew it to be true.

In fact, he was almost making this too easy, walking into the web she was spinning so neatly she hardly had to do a thing.

It was all leading up to that climactic moment when she would tell him everything, confront him at last, and throw that conversation she'd overheard at The Donut Shop back in his face.

Every single word was burned indelibly into her brain, recorded on the tablets of her heart.

Sonny Garrett was dead meat. So to speak.

Why should she feel any guilt about abusing his trust or his hospitality? By her calculations he owed her a little atonement.

Traditional Greek mealtimes were between the hours of 9:00 and 11:00 P.M. It was just past ten as Shay dressed for dinner in a pair of oatmeal-colored slacks and a matching sleeveless V-neck top. She knotted a kelly green scarf at her neck and stepped into straw sandals. One of the nicest things about the Galaxidi was that Bruno served home cooking and expected his guests to dress accordingly in casual attire. Shoes and shirts were the only requirements.

Sonny had told Shay he was spending the night in

Athens, where he was meeting his agent to sign a new contract. He had taken Buddy with him. Shay ate alone, thinking about the afternoon, and what it had felt like to be with Sonny Garrett again.

Weird.

It had felt extremely weird.

Yet, there was something oddly exciting about this sense of déjà vu. Shay wasn't sure why that should be, but it was. The fact that she knew who he was but he didn't know who she was threw a strange spice into the mixture.

It was a situation she found exciting, amusing, even sexy. Maybe it was the danger she courted, that feeling of being half in control of events, half at the mercy of whatever happened.

Bruno drew Shay into a game of darts, which she knew from past experience that he would win, so she kept her wagers low.

Shay was awakened the next morning by a persistent tapping at her door. Wrapping herself in her lightweight robe, she went yawingly to open it.

Two fresh, eager faces were on the other side. ''You haven't forgotten, have you?'' Eugenie asked.

''You promised you'd come,'' Buddy chimed in.

''Getting dressed now,'' Shay said, stifling another yawn. ''Where's your brother, Buddy?''

''Gassing up Mr. Demetri's car. We're supposed to meet him out front.''

It was just eight o'clock. Buddy and Eugenie were ready for the day's excursion. Identical Houston Drillers caps were perched on their heads. Both wore denim shorts and hiking boots. They looked adorable, the blond American jock complementing the exotic Greek goddess, their beautifully youthful faces alight with excitement.

"I won't be long," Shay promised. "Want to come in while I get ready?"

They bobbed their heads in unison, and Shay let them in. They hopped up on the rumpled bed, chattering like magpies as Shay went into the bathroom and stepped under the shower.

"We're going to Rhodes first," Eugenie announced. "I just know you're going to love it, Shay. Socrates is said to have walked the streets there, and there's a lovely beach, so wear your swimsuit under your outer garments. In Lindos we'll ride donkeys up to the ruins of a Byzantine church, or if you'd rather walk I know a stairway that's rarely used now. . . ."

Shay smiled to herself as she listened to the recital through the spray of the shower. She was looking forward to the day, though her expectations weren't as sanguine as Buddy's probably were. Or Sonny's.

She dried off, then slipped a pair of her own denim shorts over a hot-pink bikini. The shorts were too short and revealing, and she had quite possibly bottomed out morally, because it gave her a kind of wicked pleasure to parade the wares that Sonny once held in such contempt in front of him now. She added a striped T-shirt.

Back in the bedroom, Shay put on her hiking boots, and Eugenie helped her plait her hair into a French braid.

Sonny was waiting beside Bruno's car, wearing denim shorts and hiking boots. Shay burst out laughing. "Is this what you call a fashion statement, or what?" she said.

The three remaining members of the denim-clad hiking crew laughed with her.

Sonny gave her big blue cow eyes. "Did you miss me at dinner last night?"

"Desperately. I was only able to eat two helpings of Bruno's stuffed cabbage rolls." It was said teasingly, but the impact of Sonny Garrett was hitting Shay all over again. His tan was deepening visibly after days in the sun, and in those figure-hugging shorts and that loose-fitting tank top he looked like a drop-dead gorgeous Hollywood sex symbol.

For a moment Shay forgot why she hated him.

He took her hand and lifted it to his lips. The light kiss gave Shay a shivery sensation of gooseflesh.

"I have something for you," Sonny said. He produced a Drillers cap identical to the one he and their double-date partners wore. He placed it on Shay's head, then took a step back to survey the finished product. He nodded apparent approval, behind a dazzling, heartbreaking smile, at what he saw.

"The Drillers should use you to market their logo," he said. "Aphrodite goes NFL."

Shay reveled in the unmasked hunger in his eyes. She merely smiled, sweet and virtuous.

And silently cursed the blush that she felt color her face.

Sonny opened the car door for her. "I didn't mean to embarrass you, Shay. You should be used to compliments. I'm sure you hear them all the time."

"That was more outrageous than complimentary."

"It was dumb," Buddy said from the backseat.

Beside him, Eugenie sighed dreamily, and said, "I thought it was ever so sweet."

*Sonny is sweet.*

That dadgum carping voice just wouldn't leave her alone.

Shay took ten deep breaths, then a couple more.

A wave of guilt washed over her.

They drove past several small villages with tavernas and souvenir stores—and incredible views—on the way to Rhodes. Again Eugenie was the perfect tour guide, pointing out that these were popular resorts for Brits, Germans, and Italians. Greeks were notoriously terrifying, madcap drivers, and tourists all tooled around on kamikaze motor scooters.

While everyone else oohed and ahhed at the views, Shay kept her eyes locked on the winding road, catching only glimpses of flower-draped villas and rocky coasts over blue seas.

Inside Rhodes's fortified ramparts they followed narrow cobbled alleys, passing beneath numberless archways and pausing frequently to examine items of folk art sold in a host of shops. In the calm harbor fishing boats nudged the wharf against a backdrop of neat whitewashed stone houses sparkling like sugar cubes in the sun.

Interspersed among the houses were dozens of tiny chapels and windmills with thatch-roofed towers. Eugenie said this was where her sister Daphne and her husband Mikko had spent their honeymoon. Shay could understand why. It was the most beautiful place she had ever seen, almost too good to exist. A dream-like haze clung to everything.

Shops, tavernas, and sidewalk cafés were clustered around the harbor. They ate breakfast at a small side-street café, shopped for bargains in several leather shops, finding plenty—leather jackets, handbags, and shoes. They strolled more narrow flagstone lanes of the enchanted village. Even the stone alleys were white! On the brown wood balconies overhanging the street were set white pots of greenery and red flowers.

In a store where they bought cold drinks, a fishing boat was converted into a checkout counter. They lingered over a snack of tender fried squid at a taverna, where they watched a dog chase two cats up two trees, like bookends.

Guiding them into yet another side street, Eugenie led them up steep steps to a small, modest museum, where they viewed the famous statue of Aphrodite, dated from the first century B.C.

Sonny took one look at the love goddess kneeling on a knee, and rated it R. "Mama would skin me alive if she knew I was letting the twerp gawk at naked ladies, even if this one is marble."

Despite the jesting, Buddy laughed, joined by Sonny. Then the brothers Garrett decided that this Aphrodite needed her own Drillers cap.

Shay and Eugenie were laughing so hard they barely made it out of the museum.

Eugenie suggested they cool off with a swim before heading to Lindos. They rented snorkeling equipment from a shop along the stone breakwater, then drove to a beach below a white chapel.

The sand was already burning hot as they walked to the sea, and Shay couldn't resist the delicious turquoise water. As soon as they found a satisfactory place to settle, she pulled off her shorts and shirt and ran into the Aegean.

The water was ravishingly cool as it flooded around her body. She struck out toward the horizon, splashing blissfully. It was a perfect day. The sky overhead was a soft blue contrast to the water, the sunlight pouring down like gold.

The others followed Shay into the water. They swam and snorkeled for almost an hour, reveling in the sea and the natural beauty all around them. Sonny was completely at home in the water, moving with the easy grace of a fish.

When at last they were lying in the baking sun, Buddy and Eugenie strolling hand in hand in the shade of the small chapel, Sonny turned to Shay and smiled, the soft blue sky reflected in his eyes, turning them the color of the sea.

"I hope you're having as much fun as I think you are," he said.

"I don't know when I've enjoyed myself this much." Shay sighed rapturously. "I love Greece. I just know I'll come back someday."

"When do you have to leave?"

"Never, if I have my way. Much too soon."

"I suppose you have a busy schedule waiting for you at home."

Shay groaned. "I don't want to think about that."

"Okay, we won't. How about pretending that neither of us ever has to leave here, that I have you to myself on an indefinite basis." His smile was warm in his voice.

A voice that was almost musical.

The kind of voice she ought to be able to trust.

Shay glanced at him. Propped on an elbow, Sonny was watching her, and he wasn't bothering to disguise his interest in her hot-pink bikini–clad anatomy.

She fought down her prudish instinct to cover up. After all, she enjoyed looking at her new and improved body. Why should she feel so awkward?

*Stop being Mary Jane,* she warned herself. *You're Shay Benton—remember?*

*And Shay Benton's got Sonny Garrett right where she wants him!*

Shay Benton just wasn't altogether sure she was standing on solid ground.

She returned his smile. "Okay, Mr. Garrett, you've got me to yourself on an indefinite basis. But when does your reality begin to intrude on the fantasy?"

"Touché," he said regretfully, his eyes holding hers. "There're a couple of television commercials on tap, and training camp opens soon. Management frowns on truancy."

"So do road managers and publicists."

His thumb gently traced her mouth, and she shivered, though she was bathed in the brilliant heat of the Greek sun, and his touch was like a brand burning her skin. "You are an extraordinarily lovely woman," he said softly. "I find it hard to believe that you're not surrounded by a pack of hungry pursuing wolves. You must have left them back home."

"No, there's no one." Good grief, did she have to pick this particular moment to be brutally honest?

"You're kidding. Not a soul?"

Too late to lie now. "There are always men in my life," Shay said, meeting his eyes briefly. "But not in the sense you mean."

"Oh? And just what sense do I mean?"

"I presume you're asking me if there's someone special in my life."

"And there isn't?"

She shook her head.

"As much as you travel, you must meet a lot of men." Sonny was looking at her with an expression that made Shay's heart suddenly clench in reaction.

"As much as I travel," she said, "I don't have time to meet anybody. Half the time I can't remember what city I'm in."

"What about those admiring masses of fans? Don't tell me that men don't send you flowers and provocatively suggestive notes backstage."

"Sure they do," Shay said, and added mentally, *And after the applause fades away, the singer of those tender love ballads is left to her own thoughts. And they aren't much company on dark, lonely nights.*

Shaking her mind free of such maudlin thoughts, Shay added, "There's probably a female equivalent that hangs around locker rooms."

Sonny laughed. "I get your point." Then, with the smile fading, "What I dislike most about women like that is that they're so phony. Always pretending to be something they're not, you know?"

Shay was relieved that Eugenie chose that moment to join them with an announcement that it was time to leave for Lindos.

"It's a long drive," Eugenie said, "and I have a surprise for lunch."

They drove along another coastal highway. It was now fiercely hot. They stopped in the square at the entrance to Lindos. Eugenie directed them to a taverna, where the owner, a small, dark man, broke into a broad smile at the sight of their pretty tour guide, who was also the man's niece.

Uncle Alex was Bruno's brother, and together he and Eugenie unveiled the promised surprise: a large wicker basket filled with hot and cold meats, smoked and pickled fish, cheese, fresh bread, olives, and grapes.

''Papa called ahead and made all the arrangements with Uncle Alex,'' Eugenie informed the group. ''We're going to picnic in the acropolis!'' she added with a beaming smile.

Rented donkeys waited at the end of a narrow, winding village street. The party of four and their basket ascended through a gate in the castle wall. Eugenie, a talking Byzantine history book, explained that her brother-in-law was an archaeologist.

''There are ruins of a Byzantine church on top,'' Eugenie said. ''The ancient temple had deteriorated greatly by the thirteenth century, but fortunately the latecomers didn't finish demolishing it, as so often happened. One statue of the goddess Athena was removed by the Turks, then taken to Constantinople, where it was burned. But other statues have been uncovered by archaeologists working here, including

Mikko, my sister's handsome husband. The restoration goes slowly, though, as you will see."

Near the top the remains of the ancient structures were clearly visible. Beyond a row of tall Doric columns a great staircase led to the highest level, where the temple of Athena once stood. All that remained of the temple were the columns on both sides and part of one wall with a section of the upper structure. It was hauntingly beautiful.

"As you can see," Eugenie said, "the temple is only partially restored."

They rode up the vast staircase to stand on the stone floor of the temple. Shay turned about slowly, trying to imagine what it must have been like in the fourth century B.C. "It's breathtaking," she whispered, as if to speak aloud would be sacrilege. She walked around for several minutes, acutely aware that her feet fell where the feet of the ancient members of the cult of Athena had trodden. Then Sonny called her back to the present.

The food was out of the basket and on a red-and-white-checked tablecloth. There were two bottles of mineral water, still cold in their insulated wrappers. They stuffed themselves greedily.

Finally, Shay let out a gust of a sigh, her gaze traveling over the crumbling walls and partially restored columns. "This is the most impressive dining room I've ever seen. Talk about atmosphere!"

"The company's not bad, either," Sonny said, getting to his feet. He took both of Shay's hands in his and pulled her up beside him. "Let's go downstairs and look around."

He guided her down the long stairway. The relationship between them had been growing warm and intimate all day, and now they just walked in silence, not talking much, sharing the beauty of the day and the rubble-strewn archeological site.

"I hope I haven't worn you out with all the swimming and walking today," Sonny said as they stopped near where the donkeys were grazing and looked up at the temple.

Shay laughed. "I wouldn't admit this to just anyone, but I don't think there's a muscle in my legs that isn't screaming in protest—muscles I wasn't even aware existed before. And I usually jog at least five miles every morning!"

"I ought to be shot. Let's sit for a while."

They returned to the grand staircase. Shay settled on the bottom step. She leaned back, her elbows resting on the step behind her, her head thrown back, savoring the breeze that had sprung up. She closed her eyes. "This is heavenly," she said dreamily. "I wish I could stop time right here."

She felt Sonny's fingers touch her hair, caressing the salt-stiffened tangles gently. She half opened her lids languidly, looking up at him.

"This is what I like about you," he said.

"You like my awful hair?"

"Your beautiful hair." He was leaning over her, smiling down at her. Shay was so taken by the warmth of that smile, the comfort it offered, that she seemed to have lost the reflexes needed to bring everything back into sharp focus. She was barely able to remember her name. Despite the threat his flirting posed, she was now looking into the eyes of a boy who had just opened the one Christmas present he ever in his whole life wanted—her.

The relaxed mood they had shared during the day was suddenly shot through with an electricity so powerful that Shay almost cried out.

His fingers trailed down the skin of her cheek to trace the delicate arc of her jawline. "Your skin is the color of gold," he murmured. "Yet it's got an almost pearly quality, fincr than the finest silk that was ever spun."

"I think you've been in the sun too long," Shay said, trying to ignore the long fingers caressing her neck.

Sonny shrugged. "I think I read that line in a book, or maybe I heard it in a movie."

"A very bad movie."

"How're your legs?"

"Better." His caresses were not having a soothing effect on her. He smoothed her perspiration-damp hair away from her face with infinite gentleness, then slipped his hand beneath her hair to massage her neck.

Unlike the women she had created in song, Shay

did not possess an unlimited supply of playful witticisms, and she had flunked Romantic Repartee 101. She racked her brain, but all she came up with was, "We must have walked twenty miles today." Her voice came out ragged this time, almost like a croak. She cleared her throat.

"Hee-haw," said one of the donkeys.

Sonny did not answer, but bent slightly to touch her lips with his own.

A touch. No more. The velvety warmth was there on her mouth, then gone. Her insides felt as if they were turning over as a betraying weakness crept in.

Shay felt her lips part, her eyes closing with the reaction that had swept across her skin.

"You've got goose bumps," Sonny said softly, his fingers trailing down her arms where the fine hair was standing on end. Like she needed him to tell her that!

The extraresponsive condition of her skin made his touch something between torment and ecstasy. Shay felt his lips touch her forehead, drifting down her eyelids. Her carping voice tried to get through with a five-alarm warning, but at least one, possibly all, of her brain terminal wires had short-circuited at roughly the same time that their lips made contact.

The warm moisture of his tongue told her he was tasting the sea salt on her temples. Shay shuddered involuntarily. She was in the grip of a kind of sweet hypnosis, immobile on that ancient step, while Sonny kissed her face, his mouth never touching hers, drawing close, then moving away with maddening deliberation.

When at last her lips touched his, Shay knew that it had been her own movement. She lifted her mouth to his, and felt him kiss her there, his arm sliding around her to draw her close for a dizzying moment. Then he drew away as though trying to discipline them both.

"I've been dying to do that all day," he whispered. He kissed her cheeks, her eyelids, his mouth moving down her throat to find the hollow where her pulse fluttered madly.

Fluttered betrayingly.

Shay's arms slid around Sonny's neck, possessed of a will of their own. *Who is conquering whom?* Her carping voice managed to squeeze through, barely.

Her strong will was failing her, losing a battle with her heart.

Shay gulped when Sonny's warm breath brushed the sensitive shell of her ear. Then he whispered her name, and she remembered Mary Jane.

Shay drew back from him and walked away a few steps. Staring at nothing, she tried to compose herself. "We'd better get back to Buddy and Eugenie," she said, in a voice that shook slightly. "And we'd better stop what we're doing right now."

Shay ran up the grand staircase on shaky legs. Sonny followed her after a few moments. "Are you angry about what happened?" he asked when they'd reached the top.

"No, and nothing happened!" Shay said, rather tensely. "But I don't want it to happen again."

*Liar, liar, pants on fire,* that sadistic carping voice chanted mockingly.

Later, when she was alone in her room, Shay could no longer pretend that it was all just a mischievous game anymore.

Sonny Garrett was ripe for the picking. No doubt about that. Each act of the play couldn't have gone better if she'd handed Sonny a script. The man who had evolved from the boy who had once treated her like compost now desired her.

Boy, did he ever—big-time!

So where, she wondered, was all the delicious enjoyment she was supposed to feel?

Nothing was working out as simply and as neatly as she had expected.

And it was more than her unplanned reaction to Sonny's touch, when he held her in his arms and kissed her as she had never been kissed before.

Much, much more.

There was an underlying pain that was rooted in a certain day in Cap Rock, Texas. That old sharp pain of knowing Mr. butter-wouldn't-melt-in-his-mouth Garrett didn't care one whit for who and what Mary

Jane was inside. That everything else was irrelevant to looking good.

She had been on both sides of the fence now, and she couldn't decide which was worse: being humiliated because of her appearance or being desired for it.

There was the possibility that Sonny cared about her, cared about who she was inwardly.

If only she could believe that then today would have been one of the happiest days of her life, instead of a moment of acute, bittersweet irony.

Shay knew her own feelings. They ran deep and strong. Though she had never committed herself to anything other than her career, she had always known that when she did fall in love it would be forever. Her songs reflected her old-fashioned values, her ambitions of having, in the same man, her only lover, husband, and partner for life.

That was part of her. That was who she was inside, and she felt with deep pain that she could never survive a casual affair, especially not with Sonny Garrett.

From her vantage point, there certainly were no guarantees that their relationship had any prospects other than those of a pleasurable summer romance.

In her mind, Shay tried fitting Sonny into her life back home, just to see what the combination might deliver.

But how could she think of a future with Sonny when everything was based on lies and deception?

*I should have told him who I was at the start.*

A little late to cry over spilled milk.

She could lay all her cards on the table now.

Sonny's own words seemed to settle that debate: *What I dislike most about women like that is that they're so phony. Always pretending to be something they're not.*

If they handed out awards for Phony of the Year, Shay Benton would win the trophy.

*So what do I do now, Mary Jane? You got me into this mess to begin with.*

That obnoxious carping voice she couldn't ditch cast a vote for a full confession—and let the chips fall where they might.

The thought that Sonny would react with fury, or with disgust, or reject her completely, terrified Shay.

Then, in a final run through her limited package of options, she realized that, for the moment at least, she was still the dealer. And if she played all her cards right, up to the final hand, she just might be able to leave Sonny so dazzled that there would be no way he could forget three weeks of heaven.

Or Shay Benton.

She had no qualms about dealing from the bottom of the deck. Not when the stakes were this high.

*All's fair in love and war.*

The decision was made. She wouldn't tell Sonny. Not till the very end. And if she could keep it to the kind of happy friendship they'd enjoyed until this afternoon, what harm was there in letting him remain ignorant of her identity a while longer?

If Sonny really cared about her it would work itself out.

Somehow.

If he didn't . . . well, Mary Jane would have had a measure of revenge, and Shay could console herself with the memory of three weeks of heaven.

And write another song.

## *Chapter Five*

With Eugenie again serving as their expert tour guide, the Texas tourist trio visited a pottery factory where members of the same family had been fashioning and painting pottery by hand for generations. They sojourned to crumbling Byzantine churches, archaeological sites, saw ancient stone houses sprinkled down both sides of a steep hill, prowled through a recently uncovered monastery by candlelight.

They took the island ferry cruise through the beautiful gulf, an inlet of the Aegean, and around peninsulas stretching in long zigzag lines as irregular green jewels.

They spent a day at a Peloponnisos port city, where they partook in a smorgasbord feast at one of the popular hostels, while the proprietor strolled around with a loud wheezy accordion playing a punishing version of "Qué Será Será." What will be, will be.

*So true,* Shay thought.

There was more awe-inspiring scenery at a small mountain village tucked in a valley below soaring pinnacles of gray stone topped with precariously situated monastaries. They ate at a former Turkish bath that had been turned into a restaurant, lying secreted behind a dark blue door and glowing with about thirty-five dimly lit tables under the beams of the ceiling twenty feet overhead.

Sometimes they just lay on the beach, talking and laughing. They explored Kolpos itself, a red-roofed tumble of buildings and lazy pleasures, with typically narrow winding streets, sweet little churches, cascades of flowers and liquid light.

Although it wasn't easy, Shay managed to avoid any potentially compromising situation with her safety-in-numbers theory. She suspected there were times when Buddy and Eugenie would have appreciated a little less togetherness. But Shay figured they were much too young to be on their own, anyway. And she knew full well the devastating physical effect Sonny could have on her, given the opportunity.

It had gone way beyond the toe-curling stage long ago.

Her reserve clearly frustrated Sonny; he obviously had in mind a more sensual relationship.

When he asked Shay to have dinner with him one

night—just the two of them at a harbor restaurant Eugenie highly recommended—an alarm light in the back of Shay's head blinked in colorful caution: *Don't do it. Uh-uh, no way!*

She wore a slinky silk Chanel sheath, the neckline draped in front, the back deeply V'd with lapels; it was short enough to reveal a devastating length of honey-colored legs, ending in high-heeled pumps that were the same racy red color of the dress.

*You're asking for trouble, sister, begging for it,* her carping voice continued.

Perhaps. But this was her last night in Greece.

Her suitcases were almost completely packed. A rental car was booked to take her to the Athens airport at seven o'clock tomorrow morning. She had settled accounts with Bruno. She had given Eugenie one of the beautiful hand-painted vases she'd bought at the old factory as a token of appreciation. She had phoned J. T. to give him her arrival time in Nashville, and asked him to bring Obadiah to the airport with him. Tomorrow night she would sleep in her own bed with that lovable Lhasa.

Sonny didn't know any of that.

Shay checked the small, cozy room again, the drawers and closet, to be sure she hadn't forgotten anything. She returned to the mirror to darken her lashes with mascara, brushed her hair vigorously, then clipped it back with a rose barrette. She decided against wearing jewelry. A final glance in the mirror confirmed that she looked just as she wanted to look. The image was right.

Sonny would be dazzled.

He was waiting in the foyer, in a lightweight white sport coat over a blue crepe shirt open enough at the throat to reveal a hint of curly bronze chest hair farther down. His hands were thrust into the pockets of his navy trousers.

Shay gulped and took a deep breath. Then another.

He looked gorgeous enough to make her heart miss a beat. Yet part of his charm, Shay acknowledged to herself, was that he seemed to be oblivious to his astonishing good looks. He was undoubtedly attractive to women of all ages, with his hint of recklessness. There was a lively cheerfulness about him, a friendliness in his eyes.

Shay had thought she had known Sonny Garrett. She was beginning to think she didn't know him at all. Not well, anyway. He was different from other people, and she was willing to believe that he was a nice person, inside, where it counted.

Almost willing to believe.

She descended the stairs slowly and walked toward him, keeping her expression neutral. Sonny turned and saw her; his eyes widened slightly as they took in her face, then drifted down her figure.

"Hi," she said when she reached him. She gave him a half smile. "Warm evening, isn't it?"

"Uh . . . very warm. Shay, you look—"

She tilted her head. "Yes?"

"Come on," he said, shaking his head slightly. As he opened the front door for her, he touched the cool skin of her arm. "Shay," he said quietly, "you are lovely."

"Thanks," she said jauntily. "You clean up pretty good yourself, Garrett." Sonny's almost tense expression told her how completely she had succeeded in her intentions. She let a slight smile play across her mouth. "Are we going to stand here all night, or shall we go and eat?"

It was four o'clock in the morning, and the warm purple night brooded with a mist of stars on Kolpos as they walked toward the Galaxidi. In a very few hours Shay would be on her way back to Nashville.

She didn't want to think about that.

She and Sonny didn't talk, but it was a comfortable silence. A delicious breeze rippled through the ghostly trees surrounding the town, bringing with it the heady scent of orange blossoms, pine, jasmine, and the sea—a scent that was Greece.

It had been a night of magic and enchantment. They had dined on baked red snapper under white trellises heavy with purple grapes, with a marvelous view of the small harbor, the water studded with yachts. After dinner they sat by the pier and watched the nightly promenade of elderly couples and teens, families and friends, strolling, flirting, eating ice cream, and generally taking a holiday.

From there they moved on to one of the popular tavernas, where they drank retsina and listened to *santuri* music. One after another, the men got up and did the *zeinbekkos* and the *khasapikos,* in a state of exuberance that caused them to forget their surroundings and whirl around by themselves for sheer joy.

Sonny thought about joining them, then decided to wait on a two-step number, instead of making a big fool of himself, and risking injury to boot. "I'd hate like heck to have to explain that one to my coach."

When at last the band played a slow song, Sonny had asked Shay to dance, and they blended together as one floating cloud, his arms around her, tighter than need be.

They swept around the room, and the other couples passed in a blur of motion, an ocean of light. The music stopped, but Sonny just slowed down. He pulled Shay yet closer. Another song started. His hand pressed firmly against the small of her back. She caught a faint whiff of his cologne, and felt a little dizzy.

Shay no longer tried to fool herself about her reaction to Sonny; he was sweeping her off her feet, and she loved it! She loved being held in his strong arms, losing herself in the bliss of snuggling up to his big, powerful chest. Loved talking to him, listening to him. She especially loved his chin.

The chin Mary Jane had spent hours mooning over, in another lifetime, it seemed.

She kept thinking how smooth it looked, without a single blemish or pimple. There weren't any marks on his cheeks or forehead, either, but his chin had looked as smooth as cream to Mary Jane. She had longed to reach out and touch it, had dreamed about touching it, wanting to see if it was as smooth as it looked.

Mary Jane had thought she'd get to touch his chin, if Sonny asked her to the homecoming dance.

It was a stupid thing to remember, yet that thought had come back to Shay while they were dancing.

She had given in to the irresistible urge to touch that wonderful chin, then brushed the hair back from his forehead.

He had kissed her—nothing serious, just a gentle contact of lips. Yet the underlying message had been plain. A question. An invitation.

A message that tonight didn't have to end.

"What are you thinking about?"

Shay didn't snap out of her dreamy reverie instantly. She sort of faded in, like a television set warming up.

"Tonight."

"Have you enjoyed it?"

"Very much."

"We can do the same thing tomorrow night. And the next night, and the next—"

Shay was silent, thinking of the packed suitcases on

her bed, the ordered rental car. She wished with all her heart at that moment that she was really what he believed her to be: Shay Benton, embarking on a summer romance with a beautiful stranger.

Beautiful inside and out.

As it was, the curtain was poised to come down on her final performance, a limited engagement, and she had no idea if there would ever be a curtain call.

"Buddy really is quite taken with Eugenie, isn't he?" she asked.

Sonny glanced at her, then smiled. "You were his first choice, but I've got seniority in the Garrett family."

"He's a good kid." There were so many emotions hanging around Shay's neck and competing for attention that conversation was not easy for her.

"He's the best," Sonny said, "if I do say so myself. Tonight was Buddy's idea, you know. And the Demetris were nice enough to let him sleep over."

They had arrived at the Galaxidi's flower-lined path, and as Shay started in to the deserted courtyard, Sonny took hold of her arm, holding her back, and said, "Do you like figs?"

His question seemed so esoteric that Shay could only repeat in bafflement, "Do I like figs?"

"I asked first."

"Yes, I like figs."

"What would you say if I said I had some in my room?"

"That it was a dumber come-on than 'What's your sign,' or, 'Hey, baby, wanna see my baseball card collection?' "

"How about, I'm not ready for the night to end, and that I promise, scout's honor and as a gentleman, that I won't try any funny business, I just want to talk?"

"At four in the morning?" Shay laughed, rather breathlessly. "Yeah, right."

Sonny drew her to him. "Shay—"

"Is this how you keep your promises?" Shay said, laying a finger against his chest to keep him from getting any closer. "Some gentlemen's agreement, and I'll bet you never were a Boy Scout."

He looked down intently into her face. "You're having a very special effect on me," he said quietly. "I don't have a clue what to do about it, but I want this feeling to stay."

Shay met his eyes, and once again felt their hypnotic pull. Her heart started to thud against her breastbone. Inhaling deeply, Sonny brushed his lips against her hair, then found her earlobe, numbing her from toes to eyebrows.

"Don't." She drew back, needing to keep space between them.

"You don't mean that." He raked her toward him again, renewing his assault on the same ear.

"Don't." She gasped the word this time, as the

hand that had been smoothing her shoulder began to caress her face, urging it toward him.

"Shay," he said gently. His breath, moist and warm, tantalizing and irresistible, mingled with hers. His hands were caressing her flanks, moving up the bare skin of her back to touch the thick tumble of hair he had released from the barrette. "You are very special to me." His voice was extraordinarily quiet. "I don't know what it is, but I feel like we've met somewhere before. That I've known you all my life. The important thing is that we don't lose one another now."

"You shouldn't be so whimsical," Shay said, keeping her casual smile with an effort. "I think that Greek wine has gone to your head."

"I mean it, Shay. I know we barely know each other, but there's something about you that . . ." He didn't finish the sentence. "You must feel that too. I know you do."

"What I feel is that it's way past my bedtime," she said, trying to sound relaxed. "So if you'll let go of me—"

"What are you trying to prove, Shay?" he whispered.

"I don't know what you mean," she said tightly. "I'm not trying to prove anything."

*This is really happening,* she reminded herself. It wasn't a song penned in fifteen minutes to fill out an album and give her a few moments of vindictive pleasure in the bargain.

And her so-called ‘‘plan’’ didn't include tumbling into bed with Sonny Garrett on the eve of her departure.

‘‘Shay, I'm not playing games,’’ he said, using the movement of his lips to coax hers apart, allowing him to lay claim to them.

With the scalding pressure of his mouth came the exquisite pleasure Shay felt when Sonny had kissed her before. The same, and yet not the same. There was more, so much more. The slow-burning fuse, ignited when their lips first touched, had done its work; the explosion was stunning. An as-yet-untapped vein of passion opened within Shay, and her muscles sagged with it.

Shay's thoughts, dizzying, fragmented, were made up of unanswerable questions. What would have happened if she had told him who she was the first day they met? What if she told him now?

Would he be angry?

Laugh?

Each of Sonny's kisses—one feathery and teasing, the next hungry and demanding, another testing and tentative—was more consuming than the one before.

She had always thought that term ‘‘fall like a ton of bricks’’ was a hackneyed myth.

She said his name carefully, wanting to experience the sound of it, wanting the full spectrum of its meaning to still the war she waged against him, and so against herself.

He murmured her name against her mouth, and his arms enveloped her with fierce passion. His lips slid lower, to the vulnerable hollow of her throat, and lingered there.

Shay's body was moving with a will of its own, drawing his closer. Her hands played freely at the back of his neck, luxuriating in the pleasure of memorizing with her fingers the unique pattern of his hair, and at the same time making him a prisoner with her own kiss.

Her mind flooded with patterns of color rather than thought or logic, like the depths of a kaleidoscope, ever changing, never escaping the brilliant circle that contained Sonny Garrett. Fear and desire struggled in her.

If he remembered her as the brainy geek he had found so repulsive, would all his interest in Shay Benton evaporate, vanish forever?

Shay Benton, country music megastar—and number one phony of the world!

All she'd wanted to do was have a bit of mischievous fun with Sonny. At least that was what she had told herself, and she did have something in mind when this stupid game had started.

The logic of it somehow escaped her now.

She had never known such perfection as the past three weeks. Something had happened to her, something far more exciting than evening old scores.

An unexpected and rare connection had taken place between them. Shay felt so right with Sonny, and tonight, as he held her in his arms, she had believed he felt the same. She had felt that Sonny's feelings for her were real, and that they had been on the brink of an experience of a lifetime.

Something with depth and beauty.

Something to last.

Shay flinched suddenly, as though a rough blow had landed across her mouth.

"Shay, what is it?" Sonny asked in concern, seeing the color drain from her face as she pulled away from him. "You look like you've just seen a ghost."

"I have," she whispered.

His eyebrows knitted together in an expression that was half puzzled, half amused. "What am I missing here?"

"Nothing . . . Oh, Sonny, if you knew how I've prayed that you wouldn't do this to me."

"Wait a minute. You've lost me." He stared at her, his eyes registering his confusion as he tried to fathom what she was saying. Then his jaw all at once clenched, and he was looking at her as if seeing her for the first time. "Are you trying to tell me that there is someone else?"

"No. It's nothing like that."

"Then what?" Sonny blurted out in frustration. "What is it, Shay? Have I got bad breath? Does my body odor offend you? Or is it a kiss-off? Have I misjudged our relationship? Hasn't the time we've spent together meant anything to you at all? Don't I mean anything to you?''

Shay's eyes unexpectedly stung. ''You mean a great deal to me, Sonny,'' she said. *More than you'll ever know,* she added mentally.

He let out a long, trembling, half-vocalized breath that fell just a little short of laughter. ''I am totally confused, Shay Benton. But I can live with that so long as this isn't the end of it, the end of us.''

''Tomorrow is another day,'' Shay said, and giggled involuntarily. Scarlett O'Hara she was not. She took a deep breath of the night air in an effort to steady the surging of blood through her veins. Every breath of wind took time away.

He offered a grin she couldn't help liking. ''I take that as a no to my original question.'' He took her in his arms again. ''I wish you'd reconsider. My room has a great view.''

Shay's mouth drew into an unsteady smile. ''You need to work on your line, Garrett. But tomorrow is another day.''

''Yes, it is, Miz Scarlett. But that doesn't explain why you're crying.'' He kissed her temples gently. ''What's wrong, Shay?''

She looked at him from under lashes that were wet with tears. Tomorrow was going to be a very different awakening from the one he expected. ''Nothing's wrong, and I'm not crying. I am tired, though. It'll be light soon. Thank you for a lovely evening."

"My pleasure, and I mean that literally." He kissed her vulnerable lips softly, cupping her face in his hands. "You're sure you don't want to check out my view?" he whispered huskily.

She shook her head. "No . . . I mean, yes, I'm sure." She turned in to the courtyard.

"Wait." Sonny pulled a flower from the tangle of bougainvilleas falling over a stone fence. "For luck." He tucked it behind her ear, and kissed the tip of her nose.

He walked her to her room. Outside the door he reached for her again, but Shay gave him a warning glance.

"I think you've kissed me enough for one night. I don't think I could take much more."

"Good, that means I'm wearing you down."

Shay smiled up at him, her eyes lingering on the fine, strong outline of his face, that wonderful smooth chin.

Then she held out the cerise flower. "Until tomorrow."

Sonny took the bougainvillea. "Until tomorrow."

Shay let herself into the room, and locked the door behind her. How long she stood there, motionless, hardly breathing, she didn't know. Darkness draped the rafters with its cloak of gloom. When Shay turned on the lights the darkness fled but left its cloak behind.

Her eyes were blurred with tears again, tears that spilled hotly down her cheeks, unchecked. Shay wiped the heels of her hands up the sides of her face in a gesture that was almost savage. The tears were gone. There wasn't time for sentimental slop, or regrets.

Sonny's smiling, guileless face was imprinted on Shay's mind, and her heart—a look that made her feel disgusted with herself and her actions.

"Thanks a lot, Mary Jane!" she practically screamed to the empty room.

"But if he cares about me . . . if Sonny really cares about me . . ."

Great, she was carrying on a conversation with herself now.

She stripped off her dress and packed it, along with the last of her belongings, except for her nightshirt, which she put on, her makeup, and a dress to wear on the flight.

She checked her watch. Almost five. Already the sky was lightening. In two hours she would have to be ready to leave.

"And there's only one way to find out how serious Sonny feels about me," she said to herself.

Shay settled at the tiny desk and pulled a sheet of the Galaxidi stationery out of the drawer. There were no more tears in her eyes as she started to write:

*Dear Sonny,*

*Once upon a time there was a girl who*

*adored a Cap Rock, Texas, football hero, and the girl tutored him through his geometry finals. She was overweight and wore thick glasses, but she had feelings, the same as anyone else. And she had her heart broken by a conversation she overheard one afternoon at The Donut Shop.*

*I will be on my way home by the time you read this. I am sorry for the deception. I wish I had told you who I was at the beginning. But it's too late for wishes.*

*I can only hope that you will understand why I deceived you, and how much it cost me. Try to forget Shay Benton's foolishness, but not her. And maybe you will remember that other girl too.*

Shay lingered over the paper for a long while, staring with absent eyes at the words she had written. Should she add something like, "Please get in touch with me?" Add her private phone number? Her address? The pen hesitated over the paper.

If Sonny wanted to find her he could certainly locate her easily enough. Her upcoming tour had been well publicized. Concert dates and cities were splashed across every major newspaper and magazine at home and abroad, and on billboard ads. It wouldn't take Dick Tracy to track her down.

And if he didn't want to find her?

Well, there was nothing she could do about that.

The ball was in Sonny's court now, the game played by his rules.

If he cared about her, really cared about her, he would find her—through rain, sleet, snow, and whatever—and they could start their relationship on a fresh footing.

If, on the other hand, he felt only disgust at the revelation, or if his feelings had never been serious to begin with, then she would never see him again. As simple as that.

There seemed nothing more she could add. After a moment she signed the note "Mary Jane," then folded it and placed it in an envelope and wrote Sonny's name across the front.

She climbed into bed and curled up under the sheet, but behind her closed eyelids she saw pictures—romantic scenes—which swiftly, and yet in vain, she sought to put out of her mind. They kept coming back, and she wanted them to come back. Yet she did not. And through it all she grieved for what might have been.

## *Chapter Six*

"I am not in love with Sonny Garrett," Shay muttered to herself as she unleashed her dogs so they might enjoy the late afternoon chasing elusive rabbits and digging for imaginary gophers. "That was Mary Jane's problem, not mine. Three weeks of sun-drenched beaches, the acropolis and all the other fairy-tale settings momentarily affected my equilibrium. That's all."

She looked up from her disjointed musings to discover J. T. blocking her path. Obadiah rushed directly to him, the Lhasa's bushy tail wagging a warm greeting. His two companions, still searching for their bearings in a new environment, held back, until J. T. performed his smooching act. Nothing special, really, but dogs and kids were equally wont to fall for J. T. Pruitt's rough-edged charm.

Dryfuss, a golden retriever, and Bruno, a bulldog, shared head pats and belly rubs with Obadiah, loving every minute of it.

"Too bad you can't claim critters as deductions on your income tax," J. T. said with his usual caustic wit.

"Tell me about it," Shay said. "With Lucy around, the government would end up owing me money every year." Lucy Marsh, a terrific housekeeper and an even better friend, also did volunteer work two days a week at a local animal shelter, and occasionally brought work home with her, so to speak. And since Lucy resided in a pet-free apartment complex, Shay had ended up with more barn cats than she could count, and Obadiah. The coolest canine on the planet had been minutes away from taking that "last long walk," as Lucy so eloquently put it. Lucy had a way with words, and always the proper amount of drama and tears to produce the same end results.

The latest additions had come while Shay was in Greece. They'd been snatched from the jaws of certain extinction in the nick of time, Lucy said. The retriever had looked like a Dryfuss, for some reason. The bulldog reminded Shay of the rotound Greek inkeeper, who shared this Bruno's lovable facial features and friendly, outgoing personality.

"You were talking to yourself," J. T. pointed out.

"I know. It's a really bad habit. I do it all the time."

"What were you saying?"

Shay decided to lie. "How should I know? I wasn't listening."

"Well, so long as you don't start answering yourself I suppose it's okay."

At six feet, four inches tall, J. T. was a set of hinges and limbs, bushy bearded, with black hair drawn back in a ponytail. He was standing on the dirt path worn into the tabletop mesa by many sets of feet, human and animal, and, somewhere in the dirt, Shay's footprints were included.

She jogged up here as often as her schedule and the weather permitted, usually with her dog. Dogs, plural, from now on. But J. T.'s idea of exercise was playing his guitar vigorously, and his L.A. background had produced a warped personality that embraced exhaust fumes and noise and conversely considered Shay's Pine Valley Ridge country estate an aberration of fresh air and horse poop that he avoided like ringworm.

And if J. T. had driven all the way out here from Nashville today there had to be a good reason. Better than good. It certainly was not just to pass the time of day and crack bad jokes.

"You decided you hate the song," Shay guessed.

J. T. shook his head. "I loved it the second I saw the fax."

"Okay, and I'm joining the mutual admiration society. Your music for 'Cowgirls' is terrific. So what are you doing here? Did Samilee finally come to her senses and kick you out on your ear?''

''Naw. For some reason my wife still likes me, even after six months of wedded bliss.''

''Go figure.'' The surprise would have been if Samilee really had kicked him out. J. T.'s sweet, adorable bride was a kooky June Cleaver whose only ambition was to be a good wife, and, in approximately three months, an even better mother. Samilee thought it was the neatest thing that she had apparently conceived on their wedding night.

In Kolpos.

Shay swallowed, with difficulty. Inside her chest her heart strained against several scars. She pressed her lips together and watched Dryfuss splashing in the pond-size puddle left by the last rain, following his breed's instinct. Bruno was watching a well-fed jackrabbit standing so still it nearly blended into the bush. J. T. threw a stick for Obadiah, and the Lhasa clutched it in his jaws, shaking the life out of it as he ran.

''I stopped by your house,'' J. T. said. ''Lucy said you were up here walking your dogs. Oh, and she said to tell you that she was going grocery shopping.''

''Good for her, but that still doesn't explain why you're breathing clean country air.''

''I decided to risk it because your face looked like broken marbles yesterday at the recording session, and I don't notice any improvement today. You ready to talk?''

Shay walked to the edge of the bluff that overlooked a spring-fed lake and heavily wooded acreage. She looked down on her three-story, antebellum-style home, the 138-acre property located a half mile away in a peaceful pine-studded valley, the dogs' leashes gathered in her left hand. A turkey buzzard scouted a field mouse as it soared overhead in lazy circles. She heard the warning cries of ground squirrels, and the singing of the meadowlarks.

She sat down in the dirt and hugged her knees. "What's left to say, J. T., except maybe what was the point of it all?"

J. T. sat down beside her. Soon the three dogs joined them, certain this human sitting activity involved the possibility of something edible. J. T.'s fingers circled Shay's arm, delivering a comforting squeeze, her best friend and his buck-up gesture almost making things better.

The boundaries of their friendship were so blurry they might have been brother and sister. J. T. knew everything about her—Mary Jane and Shay. He had comforted both at different times, for various reasons. It was a combination of the two that had burst into a crying jag on the drive in from the airport two days ago, sobs shaking her body so fiercely Shay thought she would die if she didn't stop, and was unable to stop.

When at last the sobs had changed themselves into words, most of them incoherent at first but becoming clearer as her tears began to spend themselves, she had eked out a summary of what had happened over the past three weeks.

J. T. had given her a box of tissues that was in the glove compartment with which to blow her nose. Obadiah and his two new buddies, whom Shay had only just met, had stared at her with concern.

J. T. took the stick away from Obadiah and began trailing it in the dirt and weeds. "You did carry the revenge thing to the limits of good taste, sweetheart," he said softly. "But to answer your question, the point is that you obviously care about the guy. I was listening to the argument you were having with yourself," he added when she would have protested. "You weren't very convincing."

Shay patted Obadiah's neck where he'd flung himself across her lap. "Okay, I admit it. Meeting Sonny Garrett again didn't exactly quench the glowing embers of an old flame. So what? What possible difference does it make now?"

"Maybe none. But why don't you at least make an effort to find out?"

"How?"

"For starters, why not call the Galaxidi? Ask for Sonny's room, and then you could begin by apologizing for that ridiculous note. I still can't believe you did that."

"I can't either." Shay thought of Sonny reading her note, thought of his expression, the way his face would have changed. She had once envisioned that moment with relish. Not anymore.

If that was a triumph, then it was a mean one, and one she hadn't even stayed to witness. "I must have been insane to play that kind of trick on Sonny."

"Boys," J. T. said to the dogs, "you have a brain cell–deficient mistress."

Shay let out a gust of a sigh. "If he wanted to talk to me don't you think he would have contacted me by now?"

"Speaking from the male point of view, I doubt it. You left the guy with a major slap in the face, and you hit him below the belt too. You played him for a fool. Ego and pride come into play here, sweetheart. Trust me on that. Besides, you didn't invite him to get in touch with you. In fact, from what you told me, that note sounded pretty final."

Shay thought back, biting her lower lip, and wished she could remember exactly what she'd said. Five o'clock in the morning, under the influence of Greek wine and Sonny's kisses, wasn't the best time for balanced literary composition.

Had she made it harsher than she wanted to? Had she burned all her bridges, leaving no possibility of ever seeing Sonny again?

She blew her nose into the tissues she extracted from the pocket of her jeans. "You want to walk with me awhile?"

J. T. made a sound of disgust in his throat. "Walk?"

"It's a novel concept. You put one foot in front of the other and pretty soon you're someplace else. Rumor has it that it's even good for your heart."

"And I hear that confession is good for the soul. Are you going to make that call?"

J. T. had a long stride. Dryfuss kept up with no problem, but Shay had to hustle, and Obadiah and Bruno were flat-out running. "I'm not so sure I want to apologize to Sonny. Maybe what I did wasn't very nice, but I didn't deserve being humiliated by him, either. That hurt, J. T. It hurt horribly."

J. T. slung his arms around Shay's shoulders for a moment. "You have to admit that you were kind of a porker back then."

"J. T.!"

"Here," he said, pulling two pieces of gum from the pocket of his jeans. "They're kind of stale, but they'll take your mind off your problems."

Shay chewed as they walked the circular quarter-mile trail that cut through mountain laurel, juniper, and wild cherry trees. J. T. popped a fragrant, watermelon-scented green bubble, then pointed out that Shay wasn't dealing with Jack the Ripper. "When you cut right to the chase, sweetheart, all the guy's really guilty of is bad judgment. Granted, he said some pretty crummy things about you, but that was the local football hero trying to impress his friends, and his girl."

''Tammy the cheerleader,'' Shay injected sarcastically.

''Whatever. It happens. Kids are basically cruel. It's the nature of the beast. Something else you should consider. You weren't meant to hear that conversation, and not many people can eavesdrop on what others say about them and not be hurt.''

''And that makes it right?''

''That's not what I'm saying. I'm just trying to give you a different perspective.''

''Which is what? That it's okay to say crummy things about people so long as they don't hear it?''

''No. I'm merely pointing out that Sonny was bending to peer pressure, going along with the crowd as generations of kids have done before, and will do again. What did you expect him to do, for crying out loud? Stand up for you in front of his friends? Risk ridicule himself?''

''It would have been nice if he had.'' Then, more softly, ''But I no longer blame him because he didn't. I don't even know why I carried such a stupid, childish grudge around with me all these years.''

''Does that mean you'll make the call?''

''Maybe.''

The dogs trotted down the path, oblivious.

''Are you coming back to the house?'' Shay asked when they had reached her Dodge Ram and she opened the truck door for the dogs. J. T.'s Corvette, a silver 1963 Sting Ray, was parked a few feet away.

"That depends. Are you going to bake bread?"

"I hadn't really thought about it. Why?"

"Educated guess. Dark bummers send some people grabbing for adult beverages. You bake bread."

"I do not."

"Yes, you do."

"Do not."

"Do too."

A short time later, Shay sprinkled the yeast over brown sugar and water. "Watch, J. T." The sugar sank to the bottom of the glass mixing bowl. They waited for the yeast granules to hitch a ride on the sugar and ride to the surface, exploding into the poofed cloud. "Magic."

"It's a simple matter of chemistry," J. T. said. "No big deal."

"Cynic."

"Samilee buys rye bread from a health food store. It takes about half an hour to chew one slice, and it has those pesky seeds that get stuck between my teeth. Please tell me you aren't making rye bread."

"Relax. This is my grandmother's honey-wheat recipe. No seeds. You want your own bread board?"

"I'll pass. But thanks very much for asking."

Shay stirred the honey and margarine mixture in quickly, then started adding the flour in half-cupfuls. "That's so the gluten mixes evenly," she explained to an uninterested J. T. Her words felt weighted, sinking much deeper than reciting cookbook instructions. Would Sonny listen to her if she did call and apologize . . . tried to apologize? He must be feeling so awful by now. Would it make any difference if she told him how she felt about him?

She turned the bulky dough out on the floured board, then added scant cupfuls of flour to the sticky mess, which would eventually become a viable dough. In her grandmother's handwriting on the index card, it said to fold the dough until it felt smooth and elastic, "like a baby's bottom."

Shay stopped kneading for a moment to think back to the wonderful summers she, as a vagabond girl, had shared with her grandparents. She and Grandma Ruthie had spent a lot of time in the kitchen, baking bread and "chewing the fat," as Pawpaw called their girl talk.

Her grandparents were in heaven now, sharing eternity as they had shared fifty-plus earthly years, as best friends and lovers. As least that was how Shay chose to envision heaven.

She could almost hear her grandmother's spirited voice reciting the ingredients for another recipe. This one for a happy marriage: *Honesty, mixed with a generous helping of laughter—and if you want the dough to rise, never, ever hurt his pride. The worst thing you can do, Mary Jane, is to hurt a man's pride.*

Shay kneaded and slapped, until, realizing that she

was either going to end up with one tough loaf of bread sporting a tooth-cracking crust or a solid brick, she eased up and handled the dough gently.

She oiled the bowl, turned the dough over, and said, "It has to rise for about an hour. You want a cup of tea while we wait?"

"I don't do tea parties," J. T. said.

"How about orange juice?"

"Maybe later. Come here."

J. T. was sitting at the big pine table near the large windows that overlooked the wooded grounds. A set of two prints of Scottie dogs were hanging on the wall to the left of his head. Shay looked at him oddly. "What for?"

"Just come here."

Shay shrugged and approached the table, and as she did, J. T. took hold of her hand and pulled her down to his lap. "What do you think you're doing, you pervert? You're a married man."

"You need cheering up. This is what my grandpa used to do when I was hurting." J. T. started bouncing Shay on his knee and singing a Hank Williams song, "I Don't Care." The dogs cocked their heads momentarily, then slid back into stuporous naps in sunny spots on the kitchen tile.

"J. T."

"What?" He stopped bouncing.

"Do that again." The bouncing resumed. "You know, that really works."

J. T. laughed so hard he almost dropped her.

"You're an angel, J. T."

"Every once in a while. But I keep misplacing that gosh-darn halo. Today I found it under my pillow. I was planning on trading it in for a Frisbee."

"I'm glad you didn't."

"Pick up the telephone."

Shay sighed. "Well, one thing's for sure. Whatever happens, I can't come out of it feeling any worse than I do now."

She was wrong.

## *Chapter Seven*

Shay was doing a sound check on the stage of the Paramount Theater, singing a line about good times, when she suddenly forgot the words.

"I guess I don't know what good times are," she cracked, turning around to the six members of her backup band, Texas Connection. They were country music's best, though at the moment, wearing an assortment of ratty T-shirts and dingy jeans that looked like Goodwill rejects, they could have been just a few more roadies who stayed out too late partying.

J. T. didn't join the good-natured six-man laughing team. Standing off to Shay's right, Fender guitar in hand, he gave her a buck-up wink, knowing she wasn't exactly kidding.

Shay tried to smile an acknowledgment, but it didn't work very well.

From "Wasteland," her poignant portrayal of a young writer's realization that her dream of living a happy, normal life could not coexist with her desire to produce serious work, Shay segued into the theme of the mistake of calling certain feelings love when they should be examined more closely in "Don't Want to Be Alone," the same theme explored in "This Thing Called Love." They were sad songs that she had effectively delivered before. And sad songs could heal.

Eventually.

The trick was getting the hurt out in the open.

J. T. joined her to sing harmony for "Buddies for Life," a chronicle of their special relationship. And finally, "Cowgirls Don't Cry, They Get Even," which they would be performing onstage for the first time tonight, in Austin, Texas, as they warmed up for their worldwide tour.

Shay was beginning to loathe that particular song; she kept having flashes of Sonny's face reading that stupid note of hers.

She had called the Galaxidi. She'd had a very pleasant conversation with Bruno Demetri, who was flattered to learn that Shay had named her dog after him. But Sonny was already gone. He had checked out the day of Shay's departure—in a rush, according to Bruno, without mentioning anything of his plans. Shay had left her phone number anyway, just in case. Sonny quite possibly wanted to forget that Kolpos had ever happened. But Shay would bet the farm that Buddy would be in contact with Eugenie. "Please call as soon as possible," was the message Shay left for Sonny, and went back to baking bread.

She had spent the night wondering what Sonny's suddenly checking out like that meant. She worried miserably, sitting cross-legged on her bed playing the Gretsh 6120 Chet Atkins–model guitar that had belonged to her grandfather. She'd started singing "It Hurts Too Much to Cry" until it did, and the canine corps was howling in concert.

Then reaction to her mood of loss had set in, and Shay had berated herself soundly. Good grief, she was Mary Jane all over again, hopelessly smitten by a shallow jock to whom she meant no more than a snap of his fingers. *Forget him! You've gotten him out of your system once and for all; be content with that. He was never the man for you. Don't let your head be turned a second time.*

Forcing herself to face hard practicality, Shay had gone downstairs and baked more bread—at three o'clock in the morning!

There had been several phone calls the next day—her mother, her agent, a record producer, her publicist, and various other friends and acquaintances.

Sonny didn't get in touch with her that day, or during the week that followed.

Shay had called the Galaxidi a second time. Eugenie

hadn't heard from Buddy, although she did say he had promised to call as soon as he got back home. She didn't know whether Buddy and Sonny were going straight home or not.

Shay had gone about her necessary routine with a dark sense of frustration. She made arrangements for Freddie Gilmore to care for her horses while she was on tour. Freddie owned a horse farm nearby and often filled in between Shay's hired hands, who seemed to come and go with the regularity of the changing seasons. The last one had lasted less than three months. He had quit, without giving notice, while Shay was in Greece. She didn't have time to search for a replacement now. Her schedule was tight. The concert in Austin was on Monday night.

There were household expenses and other necessary business to go over with Lucy, a four-foot, nine-inch bundle of energy who didn't look like a grandmother but was. Lucy promised she wouldn't bring home any more mouths to feed, unless the situation absolutely warranted.

Shay did an interview for *Nashville Today* magazine. She rode Judy J., her pinto mare. She and the dogs walked as often as possible on the familiar grounds of their bluffs. She took them to the vet for their shots, made sure her passport was still in order. The canine corps didn't need passports, although they would be traveling with Shay. To avoid hassles and animal-unfriendly airlines, she'd recently purchased her own nine-passenger Cessna Citation jet.

Shay and Samilee went shopping. Shay looked over a couple of killer songs that Rudy Hale, her steel guitar player, had written for the tour, and tried to think logically about the future.

The reality was that she was concerned with little else but Sonny, wondering where he was and what he was doing.

Would he forgive her?

Would he call?

The only answer to those questions was the silence that deepened day by day, as the weekend approached, nights dragging by in an infinity of loneliness and nostalgia.

Shay was haunted by thoughts of Sonny.

Thoughts of his kindness and humor, the fun they had shared.

Thoughts of the way he had loved her, ever so briefly. That was the hardest thing to forget.

By the time she had loaded the canine corps and herself into her customized Silver Eagle bus on Sunday night, Shay was resigned to never seeing Sonny again. And she was experiencing the horrible feeling that she had lost the only man she had ever really cared about.

The 1,700-seat Paramount Theater was in keeping with the intimacy emphasized in the upcoming tour, and following the concert a throng of invited guests and sundry well-wishers pressed into the crowded backstage area. Shay was the gracious, smiling hostess, signing autographs and posing for endless snapshots. After the seventy-five-minute set all she really wanted to do was go back to her hotel, soak in a hot tub of water, and then fall into bed.

Wrapped completely in white—silk blouse, fringed and sequined vest, skintight jeans, high-heeled boots—Shay hobnobbed with local deejays and program directors, chatted with the country music critic from an Austin newspaper, and ran the gauntlet of other assorted reporters.

She met the mayor and, a couple of state legislators, one of whom said that her vocals turned his neck hairs into pine needles.

"What a sweet thing to say. . . ."

The words dried in Shay's throat as her eyes fixed on someone over the man's shoulder.

It was Sonny.

For a moment, everything hung suspended. Then Shay felt a giant fist squeeze her heart tight as recognition slammed home.

Sonny . . . and he wasn't alone.

He was smiling down at a pretty, coquettish face that Shay would have recognized anywhere.

Barbie the cheerleader, a.k.a. Tammy Sue Brenneman.

Shay's stomach roiled.

Her first thought was, *What is he doing here?*

Followed closely by, *What is* she *doing here?*

Then, *What are they doing here together?*

Shay laid her hand against her pounding heart, trying to catch the breath that seemed to have been seared from her lungs. Dimly, as if from far away, she was aware of the senator asking her something.

"I—I'm sorry," Shay stammered, completely off balance. She tore her gaze away from Sonny and Tammy Sue and looked blindly at the tall, silver-haired politician. "What did you say?"

"I was asking if you'd care to have a late dinner with me. There's an intimate little Italian restaurant not far from from here, and I thought—"

"No, thank you," Shay interrupted with cold civility. "Now, if you'll excuse me, I see someone I need to talk to. Thank you for coming to the show. I hope you enjoyed it."

She left the senator and his all too obvious underlying proposition before he could reply. The man was old enough to be her father, for crying out loud—and he was wearing a wedding ring!

Come-ons, even from married men, were an occupational hazard, but Shay had been too preoccupied to see that one coming.

Her eyes caught Sonny again. Why didn't he look at her? He had to know she was here. Was he deliberately ignoring her? Was he intentionally flaunting Ms. Barbie Doll in her face to even the score?

Sonny and Tammy Sue were talking to another couple. The male half was the biggest man Shay had ever seen—huge, at least six foot seven, and he was built like a bear chiseled out of solid rock. Sonny turned to get Tammy Sue a glass of champagne from a passing waiter. He smiled at her as he put the glass into her fingers. Shay caught Tammy Sue's silvery laughter as Sonny murmured something amusing close to her ear.

Shay hoped Tammy Sue choked on the champagne.

Champagne Shay had paid for!

Shay took a deep breath, then another, and started across the room. Her heart was in her mouth, her palms clammy with perspiration as she approached Sonny and Tammy Sue through the crowd.

How was he going to treat her? Shay wondered.

"Hello, Sonny," Shay said softly. "How are you?"

Sonny's gaze swung her way, but there wasn't a flicker of emotion on his face as their eyes met. "Fine," he said with cool politeness. "How about yourself?"

He might as well have thrown a bucket of ice water in her face. "Fine."

Sonny introduced her to the other couple. The behemoth was Conner Buckley, better known as "Mad Dog," middle linebacker for the Drillers. In the space of five minutes, maybe less, Shay heard about Mad Dog's three trips to the Pro Bowl, the two little Mad Dogs at home with a baby-sitter, and baby Mad Dog, due any day.

Mrs. Mad Dog, a petite blonde, didn't utter a sound.

But it was obvious that her advanced pregnancy was taking a painful toll on her swollen feet—something Mad Dog eventually figured out for himself, and spirited his lovely lady away.

That was when Sonny added in a neutral tone of voice, "You remember Tammy Sue Brenneman, don't you?"

Shay glanced from Sonny's bland face to the perky and dimpled Barbie doll draped over his arm, and for a split second Shay was back at the Cap Rock, Texas, doughnut shop, walking in Mary Jane's shoes.

"Yes, of course I do," Shay said in a tightly controlled voice. "It's nice seeing you again, Tammy Sue. How have you been?"

Tammy Sue smiled with saccharine sweetness. "Why, I've been just fine, thank you. But you're the one with the story to tell, now, aren't you? Would you just look at yourself, Mary Jane? My goodness gracious, you have changed. I'm a huge Shay Benton fan, I'll have you know, but, I swear, you could have knocked me over with a little bitty feather when Sonny told me that you're really Mary Jane Snodgrass. Why, I'd never have guessed. Not in a million years. There's no resemblance at all. You've—"

"Dropped a ton," Shay finished for her. She laughed unwillingly, and felt a little better.

Tammy Sue laughed too—a small, nervous sound, as if she had somehow missed the joke's punch line. Sonny's icy eyes were holding Shay's as he said,

"Why don't you tell Tammy Sue about Greece, Shay . . . or should I call you Mary Jane?"

Only Shay caught the razor's edge that lay beneath the bland words.

"I don't know what you mean," Shay said numbly. She could feel her face begin to color.

Sonny looked at Shay in a way that no one had ever looked at her before, as though she were green and slimy and had just kicked his dog.

"Sure you do," he insisted. "I mean, what are the odds that two people from Cap Rock, Texas, would end up on the same beach in Greece?"

"I don't get it," Tammy Sue said, looking as bewildered as she sounded.

"Shay and I were both vacationing in Greece," Sonny started.

"Oh, now I get it," Tammy Sue blurted, as if announcing she'd just discovered a new galaxy. "You met Shay Benton, except she's really Mary Jane Snodgrass. What a hoot that must have been. Tell me the truth, Sonny. Did you figure it out by yourself, or did she have to clue you in?"

"She told me," Sonny said flatly.

By now Shay knew that Sonny hadn't forgiven her, wasn't likely to forgive her in this lifetime. Yet she simply could not resist probing further, on the off chance that she was wrong, that there might still be a chance.

She was getting her britches caught on her own pitchfork again.

"What are you two doing in Austin?" she asked.

"Oh, I live here," Tammy Sue said. "Almost six months now. I work over at the State Capitol, and naturally when training camp opened I just had to call my old boyfriend. We haven't seen each other in ages." She giggled, while possessively squeezing Sonny's arm. "I was a dumb cluck for letting this one get away, wasn't I, Mary Jane?"

Shay cleared her throat, the color starting to rise hotly into her face. "Training camp?" she forced herself to say.

"Uh-huh. The Drillers. Their training camp is right here in Austin. Over at the St. Edwards campus. Anyway, as I said, I called Sonny, and he said he had tickets to the Shay Benton concert and did I want to go with him? And, well, here we are—and I wouldn't have missed this for the world. When Sonny told me who you were I said, 'No way.' And I'm standing here looking right at you, and I still can hardly believe it's you, Mary Jane."

"She has changed since Cap Rock," Sonny said dryly.

"Boy, you can say that again," Tammy Sue said.

"She has changed since Cap Rock," Sonny repeated.

Tammy Sue giggled and swatted him playfully on the shoulder. "Oh, you." She turned her attention on

Shay. "Don't you just love his sense of humor, Mary Jane? He keeps me in stitches all the time."

"He's a real riot," Shay said.

"And you sing even better than you look, Mary Jane," Tammy Sue said. "I really enjoyed the concert. That new song you did was great. You know the one—"

" 'Cowgirls Don't Get Mad, They Get Even,' " Sonny supplied, and a trace of bitterness put a ragged edge in his voice.

Shay thought the title of that song had never sounded so quintessentially stupid.

"That's the one," Tammy Sue said. "Listen, I've got a great idea. Why don't you join us for dinner, Mary Jane?"

Sonny said hastily, before Shay could draw a breath with which to speak, "I'm sure she has other plans. Besides," he added, turning the full force of his smile on Tammy Sue, "I made reservations for two." He put just enough emphasis on *two* to leave no doubt that dinner was intended as an appetizer for the main course.

Tammy Sue let loose another giggle. She was beginning to grate on Shay's nerves. Tammy Sue left the impression of someone trapped in the Twilight Zone of eternal homecoming dances and pep rallies.

"You devil, you," Tammy Sue said, giving Sonny's shoulder another playful slap. "You move faster off the football field than you do on it. Isn't he just a wolf in sheep's clothing, Mary Jane? You keep your motor running, sugar. Little ol' Tammy Sue needs to make a pit stop before we leave.'' She glanced questioningly at Shay.

''First door on the left,'' Shay instructed, pointing little ol' Tammy Sue toward the ladies' room.

She flounced off, and Shay looked up into the tanned face that had haunted her recent dreams—that smooth chin that had been the object of countless adolescent dreams and fantasies. It was as if she had an eye inside, one she never knew about before now, and all she could see with it was Sonny's chin.

She heard the sigh she hadn't known was coming. ''I tried to get in touch with you. I called the Galaxidi, but Bruno said you'd already checked out. I thought . . . Oh, Sonny, why didn't you get in touch with me?'' she asked in a hushed voice.

''Did you really expect me to?''

''I thought that after what happened between us in Greece—''

''What happened between us?'' Sonny spoke with such soft yet concentrated venom that Shay dropped her gaze. ''You really are something,'' he rasped. ''I'm surprised you have the nerve to face me after that little stunt in Greece.''

Shay gasped slightly at the force of his anger. ''I'm sorry, Sonny. I didn't mean for it to go that far, honestly. But I found myself in a corner, and I didn't know how to get out of it—''

"You two-faced little fake." His anger, although he did not raise his voice, was powerful. "I've taken a lot of cheap hits and dirty blows on the football field, but you, lady, are the cheapest and the dirtiest personal foul I've ever come across."

"You're not exactly Mr. Clean, you know. And I didn't lie, exactly. You didn't recognize me and I just wanted to tease you. If you had any idea how much you hurt me—"

"Look, I don't know what you heard at The Donut Shop, but I would never have said anything unkind about you to your face. I never set out to hurt you. You deliberately set out to hurt me. You decided to make a fool of me, and you succeeded. You managed to fool me completely. You must have had a barrel of laughs watching me fall for you."

His bitter laugh cut straight into Shay's heart. "And all that time I thought it was my charm that was sweeping you off your feet and into my arms."

"I did fall for you, if that's any consolation."

"That's sort of ironic, isn't it?"

"Blow it out your ear, Garrett. I said I was sorry. What else can I do?"

"What you do or don't do is immaterial to me."

Shay's eyes abruptly blurred with tears, and she willed them back. One humiliation at a time was more than enough. "And I suppose Tammy Sue is your way of getting back at me?"

Before he had a chance to reply, Tammy Sue returned from her "pit stop." "You guys weren't talking about me while I was gone, were you?" she asked breezily, attaching herself to Sonny's arm once again. Her big blue eyes searched Shay's face. "Are you okay, Mary Jane? You're as white as rice."

Shay tried to stir her bruised mind into some kind of response. "I'm fine." She nodded dizzily, and took an unsteady breath. "I . . . it's probably the heat."

"It is hotter than an oven in here," Tammy Sue said. "Maybe you ought to go outside for a breath of fresh air or something."

"Or something," Shay mumbled, her eyes never leaving Sonny, who started to smile, but it was a mean smile, nothing pleasant about it.

"I'm afraid we have to run," he said. "We'll miss our dinner reservations."

"It was nice seeing you again, Mary Jane," Tammy Sue said. "Why don't we have lunch tomorrow, at the Texa-delphia? It's over on Guadalupe Street. Anybody can give you directions. They make the best Philly cheese steak you've ever tasted."

"That sounds nice, Tammy Sue, but I won't be here. We're leaving on a worldwide tour tomorrow."

"Oh. Well, that's too bad. Maybe some other time. Good luck with the tour."

"Thank you." Shay looked at Tammy Sue, then back at Sonny, appealing with her eyes for understanding.

His face was worse than angry, worse than hard. It

was placid, almost serene, as if Shay could no longer touch his heart, for better or worse.

"Good-bye, Shay," he said, now in terms of absolute finality. Then he put his arm around Tammy Sue's waist, and they headed for the exit.

Walking out of Shay's life.

## *Chapter Eight*

"Do you think Italians live to eat or eat to live?" Samilee suddenly asked Shay as they walked down the hall of the Albergo Palazzo, on their way to meet J. T. for lunch.

Shay laughed. "I have no idea, Samilee, but gluttony does seem to run amok among travelers to Tuscany. The way you've been putting it away lately I'm surprised you're not as big as this hotel."

"I am eating for two, you know," Samilee said, affecting a pout she had no chance of pulling off with any semblance of conviction. There just wasn't a real pout in Samilee, who reminded Shay of a female version of Dick Clark, the eternal teenager.

Shay impulsively leaned over and hugged J. T.'s tiny, very pregnant bride, as a mother embracing a favored child. Some women inspired songs of great passion. Samilee induced hugs; she was one of those unique people everyone fell in love with the instant they came in contact with her, including confirmed bachelor J. T. Pruitt.

Samilee had been working at a restaurant on Nashville's touristy Demonbreun Street for less than a week when J. T. first saw her, and decided on the spot that she was the girl he was going to marry.

He and Shay were having coffee at the time, and Shay had agreed that the redheaded, elfin-faced waitress was adorable. "But if I were you, J. T.," Shay had said, adding a cautious footnote, "I'd ask to see some ID. The future Mrs. Pruitt looks a little tender on the vine, and you're what? Sixty?"

The thirty-five-year-old J. T. was not amused. But he had taken Shay's advice; he called the waitress over to their table and asked to see her driver's license.

Samilee was older than she looked, just a year younger than Shay, in fact, and the love bug had claimed its second victim before the end of date number one that night.

Six weeks later Mr. and Mrs. Pruitt were honeymooning in Greece—and now baby made three. The child would be the first of many Pruitts, if Samilee had her way.

Samilee was the only woman Shay knew of who actually enjoyed being pregnant, and seemed to thrive in that condition.

Blessed with excellent health, she had had no morning sickness, no backaches, swollen extremities, or bladder problems. And despite all the risotto, sausages, pastries, and everything else she had consumed lately, Samilee was no more than twenty pounds, tops, above her normal ninety pounds. A toothpick with an olive stuck in the middle. Disgustingly cute, approximately three weeks from motherhood.

J. T., overly protective of his wife in normal circumstances, had been dead-set against Samilee traveling with him on this tour, a sentiment echoed by her personal physician. Both might as well have been spitting in the wind.

Samilee, an adventure waiting to happen, was determined that her Lamaze instructions would be put to use, with J. T. coaching in the delivery room, wherever that delivery room might be located, or what language the attending doctor spoke.

Leaving nothing to chance, J. T. had alerted hospitals in every city on the tour. The guys in the band had started a baby pool, placing bets as to when and where the happy event would occur, at five bucks a pop, winner take all.

J. T.'s sense of humor had deserted him once again when Shay offered the worst-case scenario of Samilee going into labor between destinations.

Meanwhile, Samilee had eaten her way across Europe the past six weeks, bought baby clothes in London, Paris, Switzerland, Germany, and the

Netherlands—and she had lost her heart to Italy the moment they landed in Florence three days ago.

There were two sold-out audiences in Florence. But that filled only the night hours. Samilee had converted the formally nocturnal J. T. into a relatively early riser, and together they had dragged Shay from cathedral to monument to museum at a pace that had exhausted both husband and godmother-to-be. Samilee was invigorated. Her doctor had prescribed exercise. Samilee gave new meaning to the word.

More to the point, J. T. and Samilee were good friends, there when Shay needed them most to help her pick up the pieces of a shattered heart and get her life in gear again.

For three miraculous weeks in Greece, Mary Jane Snodgrass had lived out all of her teenage dreams and fantasies. Sonny Garrett had been hers.

Then Shay Benton had wrecked everything.

When she looked back at the decisions she had made, at the way she had left Sonny with that stupid note, Shay found it almost impossible to explain her own behavior.

She had treated it all like a game, but it hadn't ever been a game. Sonny's feelings for her had been deep and true, and she'd made a mockery of them.

That night in Austin she had lain for a long time in yet another strange bed in another hotel room, staring dry-eyed into the darkness. Deep inside the pain had been crippling. The memory of that last night with

Sonny in Greece was forever etched into her mind—scenes of him holding her beneath the bright stars over Kolpos, and telling her she was a very special woman played and replayed themselves before her eyes.

It was a memory far more excruciating than Mary Jane's heartbreak, or even Sonny's using Tammy Sue as a means to settle real or imagined debts.

Shay could hate Sonny for that, but she couldn't blame him—and she could not rid herself of the tantalizing pictures of Sonny's lips claiming hers. Once again her feelings had been trampled on. But this time she had no one to blame except herself.

Finally, she had cried, as if someone had cut open her heart, while the canine corps quivered with concern around her. "I'll live," she'd told them. And, as the gray light of dawn began to filter through the windows, she had gotten out of bed, and she and her three furry pals had jogged along miles of greenbelt trails beside a portion of a creek.

J. T. had handed out his usual advice to get the hurt out in the open. Shay was way ahead of him. The poignant little heartbreakers she had penned on the plane became part of the act.

Work had helped more than anything else. Shay's rapport with an audience was as much a gift as was her voice. But it was when she opened her mouth and started to sing that she was truly in her element.

It was dealing with real emotions that gave her songs their powerful punch. Her songs came out of her own life experiences, and they hit people emotionally because they could connect with them. Her sad songs were delivered with real feelings, and she poured her heart out in the words.

Offstage, the tears had dried, and Shay tried not to think about Sonny at all. Yet memories were obtrusive, and still acutely painful.

Samilee shot an arrow through Shay's reverie. "Isn't this hotel wonderful? I've never seen anything like it in my whole life. It's like something out of a fairy tale, don't you think so?"

Samilee, the eternal teenager, wearing a pair of loose-fitting overalls over a T-shirt, her hair swept up in a red-ribboned ponytail, her clean face rosy with excitement, huge green eyes sparkling, looked and sounded like a six-year-old on a lucrative Christmas morning.

Shay laughed again, inside and out. To Samilee everything was "wonderful"—and thank goodness her enthusiasm for the simplest pleasures in life was contagious.

"Yes, Mrs. Pruitt, this hotel is something else. *Fantastic* comes immediately to mind. Straight from the brothers Grimm . . . that's the German folklorist guys, not Randy Travis's new opening act."

Samilee giggled, which suited her much better than a lame pout.

The Albergo Palazzo was perched high on a hill overlooking the low, cultivated hills and red-tile roofs of Siena. A handsome new hotel in an ancient building, the fifteenth-century stone palazzo had kept its traditional winemaking business and cellars below, and on the upper two floors it had fifteen rooms. Texas Connection slept two to a room. Shay and her canine corps occupied one of the two suites. J. T. and Samilee were in the other.

The long, cool halls, white-walled and floored with red tiles worn to a patina, were as inviting as the large guest rooms, with dark wood-beamed ceilings and comfortable, slightly spare modern furnishings. Someone knew how to modernize this magnificent building without spoiling it, Shay thought.

Removed from Florence, its site-crammed regional capital, Tuscany had resisted the sameness that crept across borders, a downside of globalization that could make a Berlin avenue indistinguishable from one in Los Angeles. Tuscany was a place simply to wrap oneself in, though there were specific sites to see, most on Samilee's crowded agenda—cathedrals containing saints' remains, elaborate marble facades, a palatial, black-and-white-striped duomo and Gothic paintings in the Museo Civico.

However, at the moment traveler Samilee Pruitt was looking no farther than her stomach; she had discovered a "wonderful" pizzeria yesterday.

"Who'd J. T. have an appointment with?" Shay asked as Samilee set a brisk pace down a vertiginous, twisting path that, in Shay's opinion, could only be appreciated by eternal teenagers and mountain goats. It was bordered by vineyards on one side, small trees covered with orange persimmons on the other, both contributing to the sense of actually being in another world.

"I don't know," Samilee said, with no shortness of breath to mar that engaging Tennessee accent. Mother and child were doing fine, Shay noted, her concerns for the pregnant toothpick almost equaling J. T.'s. "He just said it was business and that we should meet him for lunch at one."

There was a medieval wall angling across the landscape. They passed the Museo Civico, one of Samilee's must-sees, crossed the Piazza del Camp, encircled by buildings of the dusky pinkish brown that Samilee swore gave the Crayola color its name.

"How do you know all that stuff?" Shay asked, truly amazed. Samilee was a walking, talking travelogue.

"I do a lot of reading. Come on, slowpoke. Let's pick up the pace. I'm starving!"

"We're practically running now, Samilee. And how can you possibly be starving? You had a huge breakfast, and you put away enough panforte and espresso to sink a battleship just before we left the hotel."

"I'm eating for two, remember?"

"Good excuse for pigging out."

They both giggled.

The pizzeria was located on Siena's Via di Pantaneto. It had plastic chairs and empty walls. "When you said 'Come as you are,' you weren't kidding, were you?" Shay said as they pushed their way through the crowded entrance. She was still wearing the sweats she'd put on for walking with the canine corps earlier in the morning. "It's quite possible that we're overdressed, Samilee."

"I know it's not much to look at, but they serve mouth-watering homemade pasta with butter and fresh sage. . . . Oh, there's J. T. over by the windows. Would you check out the guy who's with him? Talk about your basic hunk! Wonder who he is?"

Shay paused in shock as she registered the incredulous reality of the "hunk" sitting beside J. T., laughing quietly over some joke. A cold wave of reaction gave Shay gooseflesh, which quickly dissolved in the heat of a rolling tide of anger that was pushed forward by a deep sense of betrayal. "Okay, Samilee, suppose you tell me what's going on. If this is your idea of a joke, it's not funny. What is Sonny Garrett doing here with J. T.?"

Samilee just stood there for a moment, gawking at Shay, if questioning what she'd heard. Then, as understanding began to dawn in her eyes, she shook her head frantically, and practically bawled out a denial. "Shay, you can't believe that I'd do something like that behind your back. I'm as much in the dark as you are. I didn't even know that was Sonny until you said so. And I had no idea he'd be here, or why he is. You've got to believe that."

"I do." Shay had to. Samilee was no better at lying than she was at pouting. "You're off the hook, Samilee, but your husband is a different story. Him I could cheerfully strangle, except I wouldn't want to deprive my godchild of a father."

"I'm sure there's a good explanation."

"There had better be." Shay lifted her head in an unconscious gesture of defiance, the famous Shay Benton corkscrew curls rippling down over her shoulders as she led the way to the table occupied by the unlikely duo.

J. T. kissed Samilee's cheek as she sat down, but his gaze was on Shay, his eyes pleading for either understanding, forgiveness, or mercy, or perhaps a combination of the three.

Shay fixed him with a venomous look in return that effectively delivered the unspoken message that she wasn't ready to do any of the above at the present time.

"Enjoying your lunch, Mr. Pruitt?" Shay asked sarcastically.

"I can explain, sweetheart," J. T. said.

Shay sat down opposite Sonny, her arms crossed across her chest. "I'm listening, and this had better be good." She took her eyes off J. T. long enough to glance at Sonny, who did indeed fit into the "hunk" category of men. He was wearing jeans and a Drillers

T-shirt identical to the one he had had on the first time she saw him on a beach in Greece—a lifetime ago. "This is amazing. We keep bumping into each other in the strangest places. I'd ask how you are, but I really don't care." There was bitterness in Shay's voice. "What are you doing here? Is Tammy Sue making another pit stop?"

"Collide with an iceberg on the road, did you?" Sonny asked. "They can be hazardous at this time of the year."

"No. No iceberg. I just don't enjoy being treated like dirt."

For a split second she thought he was about to apologize. But no. He said, "I don't want to be here any more than you want me to be. But it is nice to know that you have some idea of how I felt when I discovered your asinine little plot for revenge."

Shay, having no better answer ready on the spur of the moment, said, "What are you doing here?" again. And followed it up with, "Do you want to kick one of my dogs this time?" That came out sounding like an expletive.

Samilee laughed. A short bark.

"Are you through?" Sonny asked Shay.

"No. What you did to me that night in Austin stinks, Garrett."

"Really." Sonny's eyebrows lifted. "And I suppose what you did to me in Greece ranks as a walk in the park."

"You got what you deserved, and Mary Jane and I enjoyed every minute of it! You really did make a complete fool of yourself, you know."

Shay was ashamed of the way Sonny's eyes flickered when she said that, but at the same time she was bitterly grateful. She hadn't meant to say it. Her temper got the better of her and the word just leaked out before she could stop them—perhaps because she was horribly aware that her feelings for Sonny hadn't altered one iota. If anything they had only intensified over the weeks. To have him so close, with that unreadable expression in his eyes, was something close to torture.

And she'd die before ever confessing that!

"Stop it!" J. T. snapped at her. "If you want to be a jerk, Shay, do it on your own time."

Shay looked at him, wounded by his tone of voice, wanting to say something childish like, *He started it,* or *He had it coming.* Instead, she said, "I believe you were about to explain why we're sitting here having this conversation?"

"It's business," J. T. said. "And before you jump all over me again, just shut up and listen. This is none of my doing. Hal and Jay cooked this up. I'm merely the messenger."

It was Shay's turn to gawk now, as J. T. delivered the message.

Hal Chase and Jay Bary—Shay's agent and publicist, respectively—had come up with the idea of turning the concert scheduled for tomorrow night at the Teatro Comunale del Giglio in Lucca into a benefit, with all house receipts going to the World Aid Team for Children, Shay's favorite charitable endeavor. She often helped raise funds and awareness for the organization that provided assistance to children in war-torn countries. And she wouldn't have batted an eye this time, except . . .

"It seems that Hal had lunch with Sonny's agent," J. T. continued.

"Les Lillis," Sonny supplied.

"And," J. T. resumed, "the fact that both their star clients are members of WATFC came up. Don't ask me why or how, because I have no idea. But the bottom line is that the Drillers are over here to play the Cowboys in an exhibition game this weekend, and all the arrangements have been made for the two of you to appear together onstage tomorrow night. The WATFC has already been notified, incidentally, so there's no way for either of you to get out of it unless you don't mind being branded a Grinch."

"I can handle it," Shay said stubbornly.

"So can I," Sonny replied in the same tone of voice.

"Good," J. T. said. "And I hope you can both still say that with feeling after I tell you that you'll be traveling to Lucca together this afternoon."

"He's going on the bus with us?" Shay asked.

J. T. shook his head. "No, sweetheart. You're going

in his car with him. We all are, as a matter of fact. I sent the band and crew on ahead to get everything set up. We'll meet them there.''

Shay looked at Sonny. ''I hope you're in a limo.''

''Not even close. It's a rental. About the size of the one we borrowed from Bruno.''

''In that case,'' Shay said, ''I hope you like dogs. I've got three, one the size of a small horse.''

''Does he have bad breath?''

''Only after he eats garlic.''

''Does he bite?''

''Only football players.''

Sonny picked up a spoon and thoughtfully swirled the cubes in his iced tea. Then, slowly, his eyes met Shay's. ''J. T. told me exactly what you did overhear that day at The Donut Shop.''

''J. T.'s got a big mouth.''

''Does your dog really bite?''

''I guess you'll find out, won't you?''

Sonny took a sip of his tea. ''Somehow I don't think spending a couple of hours in a car the size of a postage stamp with a man-eating dog was what my coach was talking about when he said we'd have the time of our lives in Italy.''

''And don't forget an expectant mother,'' Samilee said.

Sonny burst out laughing, and J. T., Samilee, and then Shay joined him.

## *Chapter Nine*

Passing low wooden arbors tangled with grapevines, Shay suddenly glimpsed the fat, purple fruit hanging heavily and glowing like garnet chandeliers.

Not surprisingly, from the backseat Samilee said, "Would you look at that, people? I've never seen such big grapes in my entire life. Bigger than big. Huge! Aren't they just wonderful? I can practically taste them from here. Do you suppose anyone would mind if we picked a few? I'm starving."

"I believe that's called grand theft, or something," J. T. said. "I'll buy you all the grapes you can eat when we get to Lucca. That way I won't have to visit my beautiful pregnant bride in jail."

Samilee giggled. "You really are nuts about me, aren't you, Mr. Pruitt?"

"Can't help myself, Mrs. P. It's your hair. It drives me wild."

"Oh, gee, they're at it again," Shay said with mock disgust as the familiar smooching sounds rose from the cramped backseat, in concert with the heavy breathing of the canine corps, none of which were tolerating the heat well.

Bruno, pressed against Samilee's thigh, was wheezing through his pug nose like a long-distance runner who'd ignored the surgeon general's warnings on the dangers of smoking. Dryfuss, fully extended between Shay and Sonny on the front seat of the claustrophobic, un-air-conditioned car, was panting an allegro beat, tongue lolled out, drooling all over Sonny, who was holding Obadiah on his lap; the Lhasa was currently suffering from an advanced case of foul personality disorder.

"He gets that way when he's hot," Shay said, not quite smiling as Obadiah let loose a threatening growl that had been building for several miles. It was aimed at Sonny, who had had the audacity to move a leg.

"Thanks for the warning," Sonny said with soft sarcasm. "You might have mentioned it sooner."

Shay barely managed to suppress a giggle while watching Sonny's laborious efforts to shift gears with one hand, balance the cranky Lhasa on denim-covered legs soaked with Dryfuss's saliva, and hang on to the steering wheel as he negotiated a rutted dirt road that was better suited for an ox and wagon than the invention of the automobile, assuming this postage stamp qualified as such.

"I would have," Shay said, "if it had occurred to me. And I probably should have clued you in on Obadiah's tendency for getting carsick unless he sits on the driver's lap. I have no idea why that makes a difference. Even my vet can't explain it. But it works. Hope you don't mind."

"Mind? Why should I mind? Just because he's shedding? Oh, and have I mentioned that he's got fleas? And while we're on the subject, that horse of yours should be required by law to register his tongue as a lethal weapon."

"Don't pay any attention to him, guys," Shay said to the canine corps. "He's just grumpy because we're lost and he's too stubborn to admit it." This probably wasn't a good time to be pulling his chain, but Shay simply could not resist.

"I'm not lost," Sonny insisted, and took his eyes off the narrow, bumpy road long enough to give Shay a rather forbidding frown, as if he were daring her to contradict him.

Shay could never resist a dare. "Okay, Christopher Columbus, if we're not lost then why is it that those grapes we just passed are the first signs of life I've seen since we left the main highway? You are aware, are you not, that we haven't passed a town for miles, or even so much as a house."

Sonny made a little click of impatience in his throat. "That's why it's called a shortcut."

"A shortcut by whose definition?"

"According to the map your horse ate several miles back."

"Lay off Dryfuss, Grumpy . . . and what difference does it make, anyway? The map was in Italian, and you were reading it upside down, which means, of course, that we could be anywhere."

"I was not reading it upside down, and I know exactly where we are."

"Yeah, lost." Shay shot him her best manufactured grin, the one she wore around particularly obnoxious reporters and the overzealous fans who thought nothing of invading her privacy. Sometimes she even hauled it out for her agent. "Boy, you really are touchy, Garrett. Sorry, I didn't mean to trample over that fragile male ego of yours again."

Sonny's mouth twitched, indicating, Shay thought, that he had taken a hit, but didn't want to admit it. "Isn't that a little like the pot calling the kettle black, Mary Jane?" he asked, almost pleasantly.

"For crying out loud," J. T. cawed. "Would you two give it a rest? You've been sparring since we left Siena, and you're beginning to grate on my nerves."

For a second, they did stop talking. Then Sonny, who'd been about to say something, cast his eyes downward for a moment, as if he expected Obadiah to give him a reason to continue, and inside Shay's chest her heart strained against several scars, fresh and old.

The pain she'd thought she had managed to get above kept coming back, like cramps. She pressed her lips together and looked out the window, at towering trees and greenery sprouting defiantly from decaying stone, and felt like she was a long way from anywhere.

"I'm still hungry," Samilee said, breaking the lengthening silence.

"Come to think of it, so am I," J. T. said.

"Me too," Shay said. "And Dryfuss looks like he could eat roadkill. What about you, Garrett?"

They hit a bump and the car rattled terrifically. Sonny flew up and off the seat, his head bumping the ceiling, and Shay heard a muffled growl as Obadiah's head hit the bottom arc of the steering wheel.

"Bathing isn't a major priority for you with these dogs, is it?" Sonny said.

"What?" Shay exploded.

J. T. intervened before she could work up a full head of steam. "It's not the dogs, Sonny. It's my wife's new shoes. For some reason they're kicking up a stench that is practically visible. Sorry, babe," he said to a startled Samilee as he tossed the offending sandals out the window. "But it was either that or risk asphyxiation. I'll buy you a new pair in Lucca."

"If we ever get there," Shay muttered.

"Don't start that again," Sonny warned. He gave Shay a sidelong glance. She stuck her tongue out, eyes closed, fingers twiddling in her ears. Sonny laughed out loud. "Very mature, beanhead."

"What did you call me?"

Sonny looked into the mirror outside his window with a sheepish grin. "Sorry about that. It just slipped out. Beanhead is Buddy's favorite put-down these days. But you'll have to admit that Beanhead Benton does have a nice ring to it."

J. T. tried it on for size. "Beanhead Benton." He nodded. "Sonny's right, sweetheart. That is downright musical."

"Maybe you should rename the act Beanhead Benton and the Bops," Samilee contributed, then dissolved into waves of sidesplitting cackles, which were contagious.

Shay lowered her head to look at Sonny, frowned for a moment, then started to laugh. After a moment Sonny joined her. J. T. had already caught the giggle bug from his wife.

Meanwhile, the canine corps observed their human companions with expressions that strongly suggested that they weren't traveling with the sharpest knives in the drawer.

That was comical enough to prompt another outbreak of goose honking, which eventually inspired J. T. to improvise a Beanhead Benton chorus. That led to a round of "Three Blind Mice," followed by a rousing rendition of "Row, Row, Row Your Boat," accompanied by spontaneous tittering, mostly because

Sonny kept forgetting the words and couldn't carry a tune in a sack. Shay felt compelled to advise him not even to consider giving up his day job.

Undeterred, Sonny led them through "Ninety-nine Bottles of Beer on the Wall."

Then, in the ensuing lull, Sonny requested a command performance of his favorite Shay Benton hit: "It Hurts Too Much to Cry."

There was dead silence from the backseat, save for Bruno's wheezing. Sonny didn't seem to notice, but Shay could almost hear Mr. and Mrs. Pruitt draw a collective breath, waiting for the other shoe to drop.

Shay looked down at her hands on her knees, concentrating as she did when she was trying to work through a tough patch of composition. For an instant she felt faint, dizzy, and cold, in a car sapped with heat, caught up in all the swirling emotions connected to that song.

She was almost sure that Sonny hadn't yet grasped the significance of that Shay Benton classic. Still, she felt far too fragile to pour out Mary Jane's heartbreak. Not here. Not now. It would be like exposing the essence of her very being, stripped of all pretense and barriers.

"I think I've done enough singing for now," Shay said in a moderate voice, trying to sound casual. "I'm getting a sore throat," she added, praying that explanation would satisfy Sonny. In case it didn't, she decided to change the subject. "How is Buddy?" she asked.

"He's fine. Football practice is in full swing back home, so he's keeping busy."

"Not too busy to remember Eugenie, I hope."

"Are you kidding? He's called her so many times that my dad says we now own prime stock in the telephone company."

"Good. Eugenie is a sweet girl, and Buddy's a great kid." Shay shrugged, a little embarrassed. "I promised Buddy I'd send him an autographed picture."

"You said a lot of things you didn't mean in Greece."

"That's a load of horsepucky, Garrett, and you know it. But I'm going to let it slide, for now." She gave him an angry look. He bore it, not looking away. After a moment, Shay broke his gaze, flustered.

Swiping at a corkscrew curl glued to her face by the perspiration that had long ago melted her makeup, Shay switched on the radio, then turned it off again in almost the same motion. "Did you hear that?"

"Hear what?" Sonny moved his knees. Obadiah growled.

"I don't know, but there it is again. Do you suppose something's wrong with the car?"

"It's not the car," Samilee said impishly. "J. T.'s playing with my toes."

"That's disgusting, Samilee," Shay said. "Cut it out, J. T. Right this minute."

"I have."

"Then what—?"

"Now *that's* the car," Sonny said, and the rental validated his statement by shuddering alarmingly. Sonny cursed roundly as the engine cut out altogether and the car ground decisively to a halt. He turned the key in the ignition a few times, but there wasn't even a flicker of life.

Sonny climbed out of the car, over Obadiah's objections at being unceremoniously dispatched to the ground. Then he decided it was time to take action against the responsible party, and bit Sonny on the ankle.

"Ow!" Sonny shook the Lhasa loose. "What's with this dog? He could benefit greatly from a crash course in obedience, or maybe he needs a doggy shrink."

"He has a fundamentally kind heart," Shay said dryly. She toed her way back into the black cowboy boots that had been too hot to keep on and opened her car door. Dryfuss shot out ahead of her, hit the ground running, and didn't stop until he reached a nearby clump of trees. "Pit-stop time," Shay said, in her best Tammy Sue Brenneman imitation.

Sonny looked at her uncertainly for a split second, then broke into a sunny smile that eventually gave way to mutual laughter.

"Truce?" Shay said.

Sonny nodded his head. Obadiah raced in a circle,

joined Dryfuss for a pit stop, then hauled a fallen branch to the car and began alternately gnawing on it and hacking up shredded bark. Bruno extricated himself from the backseat, and, in a gentlemanly arc, relieved himself on Sonny's Air Jordans.

"Whoops," Shay said.

Sonny merely rolled his eyes, resigned. He went around to the front of the car and opened the hood.

"Find anything interesting in there?" Shay asked as she joined him to peer in at the mysterious tangle of wires and electrics.

"How should I know? When I get past a halfback option pass I'm lost."

"I was afraid of that. Okay, let me try another question. Do you really know where we are?"

Sonny let out a gust of a sigh. "Straight from the hip, I don't have a clue."

"Should I panic, then?"

"Naw. All we have to do is wait till somebody comes along. I'll catch a ride to the nearest garage. Cavalry to the rescue."

Shay leaned back against the slightly rusted fender. "I hope you packed a lunch, Garrett, because it could be a long wait. We haven't passed another car, in either direction, since you took this shortcut. I don't suppose you have a cell phone in your back pocket?"

"I doubt it would work out here if I did, which I don't. What about J. T.? Is he mechanically inclined?"

"J. T. couldn't change a lightbulb without written instructions."

"I heard that," J. T. said as he unfolded his tall frame from the cramped confines of the useless car. "And I think I resent it. Unfortunately, it's true."

"Okay, so what are we going to do?" Shay wanted to know.

"I don't know, sweetheart," J. T. said, "but we'd better do something pretty darn quick. In case neither of you have noticed, the sun is no longer with us."

Overhead, dark and treacherous skies were obviously gearing themselves up for a spectular summer storm.

"Oh, great," Sonny grumbled. "What else can go wrong?"

As if on cue, shafts of rain hit them, soaking them in seconds. Then, as the canine corps scrambled for cover in the car, from the backseat Samilee said, "I hate to break up the party, people, but I seem to be in labor."

J. T., Sonny, and Shay looked at her through the rain-streaked windshield, shocked into silence.

Then Sonny said, "Now you can panic."

## *Chapter Ten*

Bruno wheezed. Dryfuss panted. Obadiah growled. Other than that, there was silence in the hot, cramped little car.

Samilee had had another contraction, her third in the past hour; still the rain-soaked trio said nothing.

They did have the good sense to get in out of the rain. From that point on group brain malfunction had seemingly taken over.

Shay sat with her arms around the cranky Lhasa, the remaining members of the canine corps crushed between her and Sonny in the front seat. She was thinking that wet denim and Opium perfume didn't smell any better than dripping fur.

"I had a cat once that delivered six kittens unassisted," Shay suddenly blurted. She had no idea why that off-the-wall memory, at least fifteen years old, had popped into her head, or why she was sharing it at a time like this.

J. T. laughed, a high-pitched, hysterical sound.

"Calm down, baby," Samilee said soothingly. Samilee was calmer than she had any right to be. "Shay's got a point."

"I do?"

"Sure. Having a baby is one of the most natural things in the world."

"For a cat, maybe," J. T. said.

"Her name was Sheba," Shay added.

"Who gives a rat's tail?" J. T. said in a shrill voice barely recognizable as his own. "This is my wife we're talking about!"

"I know that," Shay said softly, understanding the outburst and making allowances. Her buffer from the toughest of the tough CEOs on Music Row all these years was now faced with a situation over which he had no control, involving the person he loved most in the world. His reaction was unmanageable fear, mixed with a generous helping of self-directed anger, and probably stirred with some guilt.

Shay's exterior serenity disguised a flock of butterflies hiccuping in her stomach.

Half turning, Shay said, "Samilee, I don't mean to sound picky, but why on earth didn't you say something sooner?"

Samilee shrugged her shoulders and sighed deeply.

"I wasn't sure what it was. I thought . . . gosh, I don't know . . . that it was maybe indigestion, you know? Heck, this is a first for me. Anyway, when it didn't go away and kept getting stronger, I figured it had to be the baby."

"Good guess," Sonny muttered.

Shay started to laugh, and after a moment Sonny joined her. Then Dryfuss stopped panting long enough to give Sonny a big, sloppy kiss, and by that time Samilee was laughing too.

*Group hysteria,* Shay thought, and continued to laugh.

J. T. drew in a breath, then exhaled. "She's not due for another three weeks." He sounded as if he was talking to himself, explaining to himself why this couldn't be happening.

Samilee laughed harder. "I know, sugar, but somebody forgot to tell Junior."

"Junior?" Shay howled. "Oh, please, Samilee, tell me you're not going to do that to my godchild."

"Do what?"

"Name him J. T. Pruitt Jr."

"Only if it's a boy," Samilee said, and she and Shay were laughing again.

"The poor kid will be called Junior when he's fifty years old," Sonny contributed.

Shay unexpectedly had a mental image of Junior Samples from the old "Hee Haw" television show.

"Now that's not necessarily true," Samilee said seriously. "My brother's a junior. Johnny Jones Jr. Everybody calls him J. J. And his Johnny is Trey—"

"For crying in the sea, Samilee," J. T. practically screamed. "This isn't the time or the place for a lengthy genealogy discussion. You're going to have a baby!"

It was an absurd remark, stating the obvious, but this time there was no laughter.

Shay looked at Sonny, who was looking at her, and Samilee swallowed, with difficulty.

"I know," Samilee whispered soberly. "And to tell you the truth, people, I'm not as brave as Shay's Sheba. I'm scared to death."

She looked so tiny and heartbreakingly fragile that Shay wanted to crawl over the seat and take Samilee in her arms. J. T. did it for her.

"This is all my fault, baby," J. T. said. "I should never have let you come on this tour."

"I didn't give you any choice," Samilee reminded him.

In the palpable silence that followed, Shay mechanically switched on the windshield wipers, hoping against hope that miracles really did happen and she'd see another car on this depressingly deserted road.

All she saw was a bleak, dripping wasteland in the middle of nowhere.

Rain collided with the windshield. The wipers thumped with metronomic monotony. Rain came down in sheets, falling through suffocating humidity.

Fortunately, it fell straight down and there was no wind to speak of, so they were able to keep the windows open. The car was still as hot as a furnace.

And Junior had his own timetable.

"Hey, this could be a false alarm," Shay pointed out, breaking the extended silence on a cheerfully confident note that was as fake as her stage fingernails. "I mean, I'm certainly no expert, but that does happen, doesn't it? Especially with first babies."

"Sure it does," Sonny said. "And I might win the lottery tomorrow. But today I don't think we can afford to leave anything to chance. As my mother is fond of saying, 'Prepare for the worst, and then if it doesn't happen you're a step ahead of the game.' Or maybe that was my coach."

Shay turned to look at him. "Are you just spitting out words to see where they splatter, Garrett, or do you actually have a game plan?"

"I sure hope you do," Samilee said. Then, in a voice that struggled to be matter-of-fact and failed, added, "I seem to be having another contraction."

"Oh, my gosh," J. T. said, almost conversationally.

"Oh, my gosh," Shay repeated, though her alarm came from an entirely different source.

A big black cat—it *would* have to be a black cat!—had appeared out of nowhere, and as it sprinted across the hood of the car, Dryfuss, the only member of the canine corps tall enough to see over the dash, followed his instincts; the retriever was across Sonny and out

the open window before Shay finished her "Oh, my gosh."

Shay and Sonny opened their respective doors simultaneously. As they did, Bruno exited left, and Obadiah exited right, both alerted by their pal's frantic barking, sending the message that something out of the ordinary was in the making. That they didn't have a clue as to what that something was mattered not at all. The chase did. Then they caught the scent of a tuna breath and were gone.

Without thinking, Shay ran after them, yelling a useless "Stop" command. Sonny's similar shout was directed at Shay. She ignored him. The dogs ignored her.

The rain was pelting down in buckets, soaking Shay again in seconds and making her red T-shirt cling clammily to her body. Her jeans and boots felt as if they weighed a ton.

She lost sight of the dogs, but blindly followed the frenzied communications, easily identifiable: Dryfuss's deep-throated baying; Bruno's high-pitched yapping; Obadiah's rolling-thunder woofing that was comically out of proportion to his diminutive stature.

Shay found herself swallowed by densely packed trees. She jumped an exposed root, cleared a barrier of bush clutter, sidestepped one mud puddle, and splashed through several others. As the minutes passed she wondered where on earth she was headed. It had been a while since she'd had the time to jog, and sh

was out of condition. Her heartbeat had become so rapid it seemed like one steady thrum in her chest.

At last she came to a clearing and saw the canine corps. They were sniffing around a closed gate that was attached to a stone wall approximately six feet high—too tall for even the retriever to clear, but easy pickings for Tuna Breath.

Bent at the waist, Shay gulped wet air into her burning lungs, until her breathing and heartbeat had returned to some semblance of normal. The muscles in her legs were trembling from the run.

She walked over to where the canine corps continued to lament their failure, rubbing the back of her legs where the ache was the worst. Cowboy boots were never intended for use as footwear in any exercise program, especially running full speed through a muddy forest in hot pursuit of dogs on an important mission.

"Shame on you guys," she said, delivering the obligatory scolding. "Bad doggies." Relief and general affection combined to render the reprimand halfhearted, at best. The trio of unrepentant pooches looked up at her as if to say, Hey, what did you expect?

"I'm glad old Tuna Breath got away," Shay told the trio. "Serves you right for scaring me half out of my wits and getting me drowned in the process."

"Don't be too hard on them. They may have just saved our hides."

Shay turned and brushed wet hair out of her eyes. She had been unaware that Sonny had joined in the chase, but she had never been so happy and relieved to see anyone in her life, and tried not to show it. No way was she going to admit that she wasn't altogether sure she could find her way back to the car on her own. "What are you talking about?"

"See for yourself."

Shay followed Sonny's pointing finger, her eyes settling on a house at the end of a wide, curving drive beyond the closed gate.

No, not a house, she mentally corrected. What she saw was much too big to be classified merely as a house.

She decided on *villa*. Yet, looming somewhat menacingly through the grayish fog that swirled up through the curtains of rain, it was nothing like any of the glamorous dwellings she'd seen in other parts of Italy, or in Greece.

Shay shuddered involuntarily as she took in the tall, turreted, gray stone building, flanked by brambles and moss-draped trees, and sunken into a sloping hill, making it look like a ship run aground. "That place is creepy. It looks like something out of Edgar Allan Poe's worst nightmare."

"I don't care if there's a torture chamber in the basement. I see lights, which means there's people . . . and telephones . . . and quite possibly a car that actually does what it's supposed to do. Let's see if the gate's unlocked."

It was, and Tuna Breath had been eavesdropping from the other side.

Surprised by the face-to-face encounter with its sworn enemies, for a split second the black cat froze in place. One of Obadiah's unique barks, beginning at his bushy tail and thrusting forward in a rotating grunt that tumbled out at the other end like a wheel crunching across gravel, nudged Tuna Breath out of his trance. The cat jumped straight up, then came back down to earth in full running stride.

First Obadiah, then Dryfuss, followed by Bruno, ran between Shay's legs, and the chase was on again. When Shay hesitated, Sonny grabbed her hand and pulled her along with him up the drive. Loose gravel crunched beneath their feet, mimicking Obadiah's bark, or maybe it was the other way around; in either case Shay started to giggle, a breathless sound bordering on hysteria.

Then she got the hiccups.

The cat darted between a clump of enormous cedars, Dryfuss gaining ground, while his short-legged partners labored a body's length behind, slow but determined. As Sonny and Shay rounded the same bend, the cat zigged left, then zagged right. The canine corps stayed the straight course and arrived at a vine-covered stone veranda on the north side of the house just as Tuna Breath slipped through an open French door and dashed inside the house.

Dryfuss's entry was less than graceful; he went sprawling the moment he hit the marble floor—on his belly, chin first, legs extended two to a side in a badly imitated swan dive.

Undeterred, he picked himself up, did a couple of wheelies, and found enough traction to continue on his journey. A low center of gravity saved Obadiah and Bruno from repeating the same embarrassing flop.

"We can't go in here," Shay hiccuped out as Sonny dragged her into the house. She tried to resist his pulling. The slick soles of her boots were against her.

One good yank was all it took to unglue her stubborn resolve to stay put.

The canine corps had left a muddy trail of smeared puppy paws from the door they'd entered to another door that led heaven alone knew where. "This is—hiccup—breaking and—hiccup—entering—hiccup—or something—hiccup," Shay protested.

"The door was open," Sonny pointed out.

"Oh, good—hiccup—you can explain that—hiccup—to the police—hiccup—when we're—hiccup—arrested—hiccup. Oh, my word—hiccup—would you look at this place?"

They were in a massively carved stone library, but the carving had been worn by time and neglect, and the spines of the books crammed haphazardly in the floor-to-ceiling shelves that surrounded them were hung with cobwebs thicker than the moss on the trees outside.

The light that had given Sonny comfort and hope was not of the electric variety. An antique silver lamp burned in a corner, throwing long, quivering shadows against the walls. More cobwebs dangled from a fireplace that appeared to be big enough for a family of four to live in comfortably. The furniture was heavy and dark, very old and very worn. The air carried a slight hint of mold and mildew and decay, Shay thought, although she wasn't sure what decay smelled like.

"Oh, my word—hiccup. I think we've just wandered—hiccup—into Count Dracula's castle—hiccup!"

Sonny gave a small, breathless laugh. "You're nuts. This isn't a castle and we aren't in Transylvania."

It came out flippant, but he had stopped in his tracks, and Shay noticed he was looking around with an expression that suggested that if he had his druthers he'd just as soon have a three-hundred-pound linebacker slam him to the turf than be here.

Then, as if realizing Shay was watching him, Sonny cleared his throat and said, "So this place isn't going to make the cover of *House Beautiful* and hasn't been cleaned since Mussolini was in power. Who cares? Beggars, as they say, can't be choosers, or are you forgetting about Junior?"

For a moment Shay had. "You're right—hiccup. We've got to get—hiccup—help, even if it is—hiccup—the count—hiccup."

Sonny squeezed her hand reassuringly. "Maybe we'll get lucky and this will turn out to be the residence of Herman and Lily Munster."

"Now there's a—hiccup—comforting—hiccup—thought."

The place was like something out of a nightmare, Shay thought, as Sonny pulled her through the interior doorway recently used by the animal brigade and into a hall. It was dark and dank. Worn tapestries covered the walls, laced with more cobwebs. The furniture was faded and layered with dust. Their footfalls echoed hollowly. Sonny's feet were squishing in his Air Jordans.

"Hello, is anybody here?" Sonny called out.

Shay was beginning to hope there wasn't. "Let's find my babies and—hiccup—a telephone—hiccup—in that order and then—hiccup—get the—hiccup—heck out of Dodge."

"Who are you going to call? We don't even know where we are, and I don't know about you, but my Italian is limited to two words: Sophia Loren."

"I—hiccup—took a crash—hiccup—course before we—hiccup—left on the tour—hiccup. Oh, my word—hiccup—did you hear that?"

Before Sonny could ask, "Hear what?" the heavy steps Shay heard approaching from behind a great door off to their left blended with the sound of the door squeaking open, to reveal a man who seemed almost as tall as Herman Munster, clad in black from head to foot, without a single speck of color about him anywhere.

He was an instant cure for Shay's hiccups.

## *Chapter Eleven*

Where there there had been no extracurricular activity connected with the storm before, now lightning painted the room a momentary lurid violet, and thunder followed like a mortar barrage, as if the big man in black had brought it with him.

The sound was so close and splintery that Shay jumped, and as her mouth opened, her brain was saying *Scream*; what came out instead was a high, adenoidal giggle.

*This has to be a nightmare,* she thought. The situation was just too hackneyed to be real—vast, ruined castle/villa rising out of swirling fog; raging storm, complete with jagged bolts of lightning and booming thunder; Herman Munster/Count Dracula/Dr. Frankenstein's pal, take your pick; young stranded couple.

Clichéd terror struck her, straight from a B movie that insomniacs in Cap Rock, Texas, would watch at three A.M., between Burger Boy commercials.

*I've been standing here for what seems like hours, like a statue, and have yet to utter a single word; what's going on here? Has some magic spell turned me to stone, or maybe a pillar of salt, like Lot's wife?*

Tuna Breath came flying around a corner, the canine corps in hot pursuit.

*It's been five seconds since the man in black appeared,* the cooler, practical side of Shay's mind informed her. *Maybe only three.* And as if that logic had been all her full brain had been waiting for, her vocal cords unlocked and pushed out a rolling tide of words she had little or no control over.

"You're probably wondering who we are and what we're doing here and why my dogs are chasing your cat, assuming that is your cat, and I know we should have knocked, but the door was open so we didn't really break in—"

Shay felt the warm pressure of Sonny's hand against her neck and took a much-needed breath after delivering that unpunctuated monologue.

"Shay, you're babbling like an idiot." Sonny's words were nagging; the tone was not. He rubbed the back of her neck as he spoke. Shay wondered if he felt the chilled sweat there.

The animal brigade flew by again, Tuna Breath apparently deciding to lead them around in circles.

Sonny's eyes left Shay to look up at the man in black—and even the Drillers wide receiver, at six foot, four inches, had to look up at their silent host.

Calmly, Sonny began to explain their plight. It didn't take Shay long to deduce that he wasn't getting through; the man's blank expression was a dead giveaway.

She lowered her head and said quietly out of the corner of her mouth, "Sonny, I think we're both wasting our breath. This man obviously doesn't understand a thing we're saying."

There was a beat of silence, and then Sonny said, "Okay, Sophia Loren, you take it from here." When Shay hesitated, Sonny gave her a considering look. "You did say you spoke Italian, didn't you?" Shay thought she caught just a hint of panic beginning toward the end of the question.

Her shrug was less than reassuring. "J. T. thought it would be a nice gesture if I learned a few words. Enough to greet fans with a friendly "Howdy, y'all" in each of the countries we were to visit."

Another considering look. Then, "Let me see if I've got this straight. What you're saying, basically, is that you can tell this man you hope he enjoyed your latest CD, but you probably can't explain that there's a baby about to be born out there in the middle of the sticks. Is that about it?"

"Sarcasm doesn't become you," Shay began, and then the sky was split by a long lace of electricity flowing down in the rain. Thunder rattled the windows before the lightning could even begin to fade. The wind picked up, hissing in the trees surrounding the house.

Tuna Breath and company rounded the corner again, continuing the merry-go-round chase. Dryfuss rushed past Shay so close that she was almost knocked flat. Obadiah and Bruno blew by on the right, hitting Sonny below the shin, and before they had a chance to recover from that run-through, the cat did a quick U-turn at the end of the hall, and the brigade was back for a curtain call.

This time blackie the cat had a different strategy in mind, splitting Shay and Sonny and darting between blackie the man's legs.

What happened next reminded Shay of one of those goofy Three Stooges movies. Dryfuss, catching sight of blackie the man for the first time, skidded to a stop; in a comical chain reaction Obadiah slammed nose-first into the retriever's rump, and Bruno rear-ended the Lhasa.

Shay wanted to laugh, but didn't. Blackie the man did, an explosion Shay at first mistook for thunder. The canine corps stopped in the middle of a bark and fell in love.

"They'll get you muddy," Shay warned, forgetting the language barrier as the suddenly affectionate pooches stood on hind legs, lapping up words Shay didn't understand. But when blackie the man addressed her directly, she nodded anyway, relieved and reassured. It was the tone, she decided—that cheerful tone of voice.

"What's he saying?" Sonny wanted to know.

"I have no idea," Shay admitted. "But my babies trust him, and I trust their instincts."

By this time a woman had appeared behind blackie the man. She was about Samilee's height, which placed her just slightly above the man's belt buckle. At Shay's guess, she was in the same sixtyish age bracket as the man, a handsome woman, also in black, who might have been Lily Munster's older sister. Her white hair, knotted at the top of her head, matched the man's long white mustache. Her smile was dazzling, her voice caressing, charming the canine corps out of one love affair and directly into another.

The tiny woman motioned Shay and Sonny into a room that was totally out of sync with the horror-flick image. It was an oasis in the middle of a desert, comfortably cluttered with an accumulation of sofas and chairs that had seen better days yet remained inviting, exuding a welcoming warmth that balanced the woman's smile. The furniture was faded but still elegant in its floral chintz. Everything was spotlessly clean. The smell of pipe tobacco reached Shay's nostrils, and she felt oddly at home, though she couldn't for the life of her figure out why.

This room, Shay thought, was obviously this odd couple's sanctuary. The villa was most likely an inheritance, minus the funds necessary for proper upkeep.

The woman settled on a faded rug in the center of the fickle pooch trio, who rolled over to show her their muddy bellies. In turn, the woman scooped each of them up in her arms, cooing and clucking, though with Dryfuss, who was almost as big as the woman, it was more or less a half-on, half-off her lap proposition. None of the three offered even token objections when the woman formally introduced them to Tuna Breath, who had slinked over to claim his share of the distributed affection.

Shay and Sonny looked on, amazed. Shay felt herself smiling with the relaxed confidence of being in the presence of a woman who could handle any emergency, including the imminent birth of Junior.

Shay thought the woman called the cat Corfu, something that sounded like a sneeze. In choppy Italian butchered so badly she hoped it was recognizable, Shay managed a greeting, of sorts.

The woman looked up at her, smiled, and said something in return.

Sonny asked for a translation. "Well," Shay said, "I'm not sure. She either said, 'Welcome to our home,' or 'My toilet's not working.' "

She ignored his give-me-strength eye roll. Indicating herself, Shay said to the woman, "Me Shay." And, pointing to Sonny, "Him Sonny." Then she realized how she must sound. "Good grief," she muttered. "I'm talking like Tonto!"

She tried again. Using the few applicable Italian words at her disposal, hand gestures, and other charadelike movements, Shay knew she had managed to communicate their emergency status when instant pandemonium erupted.

"*Bambino!*" the tiny woman shrieked. Once. Twice. Three times. Her eyes grew larger with each proclamation, until they were the approximate size of Dryfuss's favorite Frisbee. The dazzling smile was gone. Now she only looked sick. She took a quick turn around the room, wringing her hands in front of her. Shay's initial image of an in-control woman was shattered on the spot.

Blackie the man wasn't saying anything. He just stood there, as stiff and straight as a board—not a reassuring kind of silence. It was more like he was in a state of shock, his eyes glazed. Shay didn't think he'd blinked since her *bambino* revelation. His face was as white as his mustache.

The canine corps and Tuna Breath all looked puzzled.

Sonny said, "Why is it I get the impression that for these two, having a baby isn't one of the most natural things in the world?"

"Apparently they don't know nothing about birthing babies, Miz Scarlett," Shay said, and started to giggle. She shoved the heel of one hand against her lips to stifle the sound. This definitely was not a giggling situation. Sonny took her other hand in his and held it to his chest.

"*Bambino!*" the woman shrieked again as she took another turn around the room.

Shay resisted a very strong urge to try the time-honored slap-to-the-face therapy. "*Si, bambino,*" she said, and just hearing the words coming out of her mouth made her feel a little stronger, more in control, although she didn't know nothing about birthing babies, either.

*Please let it be the most natural thing in the world,* she silently prayed, and thought of Sheba the cat again.

Thought about Samilee.

In Italian, Shay told blackie the man that it was time to gct it in gear, or something close to it. A few minutes later, they headed out into the pelting rain as the lightning flashed and thunder rolled. Shay, Sonny, blackie the man, who now had a name, and a new friend.

Blackie the man was Reggio Calabria, his companion a bottle of wine, no label, which left Shay and Sonny to draw the same conclusion: Reggio Calabria was an Italian bootlegger!

"Nobody back home is ever going to believe any of this," Shay whispered to Sonny as they jostled along in an ancient wagon pulled by two enormous Clydesdales, driven by a Herman Munster look-alike with a mustache who was quite possibly in the illegal wine distribution business, and who sampled the goods on a regular basis, straight from the unlabeled bottle.

"That's assuming we get back home," Sonny said. He was still holding Shay's hand in a death grip that was seriously threatening to cut off the flow of blood to her fingers, which were already going numb. Shay didn't mind one bit. She would mind, in fact, if he weren't holding her hand.

Reggio offered them both his bottle. They both declined, regretfully in Shay's case. Though she had never acquired a taste for anything stronger than the mixed fruit drink she and her blender had invented years ago, at the moment the thought of alcohol numbness did have a certain appeal.

A clearer head prevailed.

Somebody had to keep a clear head.

Shay couldn't really blame the Calabrias for their panicked reaction to having this crisis dumped on their doorstep. It made her like them better. She couldn't think of a reason why that should be, but it was.

Reggio and Riace Calabria were an eccentric couple who lived alone in a no-clock zone, blessedly timeless and stress-free. One cat. No children. No electricity. No telephone. No automobile. Shay had been able to converse sufficiently with Mr. Calabria to extract that information.

And other than the fact that they were getting drenched to the bone, Shay considered it a stroke of luck that Reggio drove a wagon instead of a car. The roads were no longer merely muddy; they had turned into a quagmire. Any motorized vehicle short of a Sherman tank would be useless.

The Pruitts were as they left them, in the backseat of the saunalike rental. J. T. was holding Samilee in his arms, her hair plastered flat against her head in a sweaty helmet.

"Did you find anything to eat?" Samilee asked as the car door opened.

J. T. said, "The contractions are three minutes apart." He wasn't crying exactly, but his voice was thick and unsteady.

Shay wasn't worried about Samilee. She did have her doubts about the chances of J. T.'s survival.

The storm was slacking as they returned to the villa, and Shay supposed that in another hour or two it would be hot and bright again.

And in another hour or two Samilee could be a mother!

All bets were off.

No doctor.

No delivery room.

Shay's worst-case scenario had come to pass.

And there was a better chance of her singing a duet with Pavarotti at Carnegie Hall than of J. T. successfully coaching his wife through this delivery!

As if reading her thoughts, Sonny pulled Shay to a stop while J. T. carried Samilee into the villa behind

Reggio, and said, "Do you actually know what you're doing here, or are you playing this by ear?"

"Nothing to it," Shay said. "Remember, having a baby is the most natural thing in the world."

"I don't like the doubtful sound in your voice. There's more guessing than knowing in it."

*He's right,* Shay thought, frowning, then looked around. She saw only the puzzled eyes of Reggio as he held the door open for a shaky J. T., whose face was parchment pale.

She turned back to Sonny. "Who else is going to do it?" she said in a kind of sigh. She fell into step behind J. T., and then halted again, distracted momentarily by the spiderweb over the door. The overhang had protected it from the worst of the squall, but raindrops hung from the gossamer threads like tiny, quivering diamonds.

"Shay, are you all right?" Sonny asked from behind her.

"No," she said, and crossed over the threshold. The canine corps and Tuna Breath, now best friends, joined the parade to a well-lit upstairs bedroom. The curtains and upholstery of the chairs and sofas were of beautiful fabrics, and Shay figured they must have been of fabulous value when they were made, for they were obviously very old, worn and frayed and moth-eaten.

Riace Calabria was turning back covers on an immense canopy bed. She seemed in control of her faculties at the moment, but her movements were inordinately slow, almost mechanical, as if she were sleepwalking, or drugged.

For the first time, Shay saw clearly how frightened the woman was. *The poor soul has probably never had to face a crisis in her entire life,* Shay thought.

Shay went over and touched Riace Calabria's shoulder. The woman glanced up, as if started out of a dream. She held Shay's gaze briefly, accepting the unspoken message of sympathic understanding, blinking what Shay translated as an apology in response.

Then, as J. T. deposited his wife on the readied bed and Samilee shuddered and howled through a long, continuing contraction, the rats began to desert the sinking ship.

Riace Calabria was brushing past Shay, bumping her so hard with her shoulder that Shay would have gone into the bed with Samilee if she hadn't managed to grab the bedpost. Mr. Calabria's eyes reminded Shay of a deer she'd seen once caught in the headlights of her touring bus on a lonely country road somewhere. J. T. had swerved at the last minute, in time to avoid a collision.

Mr. Cool had lost his cool completely this time around.

''Don't want to see this,'' J. T. said, in a kind of gurgling voice, as if about to vomit.

*''Bambino!''* Mrs. Calabria screeched, which was excuse enough for Mr. Calabria to find the hysteria zone; he spoke up in a voice that sounded both apol-

ogetic and bemused, but was too hurried and excited for Shay to make heads or tails of it. Both Calabrias stared at Shay with eyes that were almost comically round.

Alternating between English and her limited resource of Italian, in a voice so composed it surprised even her, Shay somehow managed to convey the message to the two men that, for the sake of all concerned, it might be best if they adjourned downstairs for a visit with Reggio's unlabeled bottle friend. Several, if he had them.

She didn't have to say it twice.

Reggio Calabria pushed J. T. through the door and out into the hall in front of his hasty retreat. Riace Calabria started to follow, then paused long enough to dig into the pocket of her black dress and press the extracted contents in Shay's hands; she closed her fingers around a beautiful silver rosary. Mrs. Calabria shut the door behind the canine corp as they followed Tuna Breath out of the room.

Shay closed her eyes and prayed, really prayed for the first time since she was eleven and Grandma Ruthie took her to a Baptist revival. No, that wasn't quite true. She had prayed that Sonny would ask her to the homecoming dance, a lifetime ago.

This made Mary Jane's heartache seem like a minor annoyance comparision.

Samilee howled. Shay's eyes flew open and fixed on Sonny. Shay carefully tucked the rosary away in the pocket of her jeans. "What about you, Garrett? Are you going to be any help?"

He raised his hands in front of him, palms up, to indicate he didn't know.

Another ear-shattering howl came from the bed.

Without knowing how they got there, Shay was on one side of the bed, offering words of encouragement, and Sonny was on the opposite side.

He was bathing Samilee's sweat-soaked face with a wet washrag that had plausibly come from the adjoining bathroom, though Shay wasn't physically aware of his having gotten the towel.

Samilee thrashed, panted, pushed. The baby's head, covered with wet, dark hair, captured both Shay's and Sonny's attention.

"You're doing great," Shay said enthusiastically. "Breathe, Samilee. Remember all those Lamaze classes."

"Don't want to," Samilee panted out. "It hurts. . . . I don't want to have this baby anymore!"

"Tough cookie, Cookie," Shay said. "This is my godchild we're talking about here, so push!"

Sonny said, "Remember Sheba the cat."

Samilee's laughter blended into a final guttural scream, and within moments the baby was out, breathing deeply, gathering its wind. The first cry erupted clear and loud, shattering the brief silence.

It seemed a miracle of the highest order.

## *Chapter Twelve*

Riace Calabria might not win any medals for grace under fire, but she did manage to serve a feast fit for a king less than an hour after Benton Garrett Pruitt entered the world.

Much to her chagrin, Shay's godchild was already referred to as ''Junior,'' although she figured he'd get a kick out of the story behind that nickname when he was older.

There was risotto, sausage, beans, Chianti, and biscotti dunked into sweet red wine, poured from one of Reggio's unlabeled bottles. The ambience was nineteenth-century country kitchen, complete with woodburning stove. The kitchen proved to be another well-lit, cheery room, tucked away in Dracula's castle, that reminded Shay of Grandma Ruthie.

The canine corps and Tuna Breath enjoyed a banquet of their own, minus the wine, in a corner of the old-fashioned kitchen that offered the same courteous welcome as did its old-fashioned dwellers.

Samilee had been starving after a short nap, and Mrs. Calabria took a food-filled tray up to the perky new mom.

Riace Calabria was smiling, obviously in her element again, now that the crisis had passed. The last time Shay checked, Riace was rocking Junior and singing him an Italian lullaby. Junior was swaddled in white linen—it looked to Shay like a very old and very expensive tablecloth of the kind used at elegant dinner parties that she imagined had once been commonplace at Villa Calabria, a generation or two removed.

Samilee, wearing one of Riace's nightgowns, was bright-eyed and bushy tailed, already restless. Shay had a feeling Mom would be ready to resume her sightseeing binge shortly, Junior in tow.

And Samilee had packed enough baby clothes for triplets, assuming they were ever reunited with their luggage at Lucca.

Downstairs, there were toasts galore, and everyone ate prodigiously. Then the celebration moved to the comfortable living room, for more toasts from J. T. and Reggio, who seemed to be enjoying one of those male-bonding rituals that transcended language and cultural barriers.

Both men puffed on the big black cigars that Sonny

and Shay had declined, and at different points laughed so hard that tears ran down their faces.

In the background, an Italian opera floated forth off a 78 rpm record from a windup Victrola.

"I'll never be able to repay you, sweetheart," J. T. said softly, lifting his glass to Shay.

"You already have," she said, but didn't elaborate. Shay's reward was the look on J. T.'s face when he held his son in his arms for the first time, tears running down his cheeks to meet a wonderfully goofy grin.

Their seven foot, 300-plus-pound host had turned into a bundle of mush when Shay placed the baby in his huge arms.

Mrs. Calabria had looked on with tear-filled eyes and an expression of love on her face that moved Shay's heart.

Life was sweet.

"I'm sorry I couldn't hold up my end of the bargain," J. T. added, a little embarrassed.

Shay smiled. "Nobody's going to hold that against you, and I promise not to tell. Cross my heart." She made the appropriate sign.

J. T. grinned. "And all's well that ends well."

"Something like that." Shay looked around and spotted Sonny beyond the open doors that led to a spacious veranda.

J. T. took his own look. "He's a good man, sweetheart."

Shay nodded.

"I feel like I'm a hundred years old," she said wearily as she joined Sonny on the pink brick veranda.

"Don't worry; you don't look a day over eighty-eight," he said, and smiled when she made as if to pop him. "Do you suppose we will ever be able to have a conversation without drawing blood?"

"Maybe."

"Anything's possible."

"I guess."

Sonny picked at lint on his jeans. "You were pretty good in there with that baby stuff. I mean, boy-howdy."

"Thanks. You weren't bad yourself, Garrett." Shay curled her fingers into her hair and gave a brief, hard tug, as if to assure herself that she wasn't dreaming, after all, that the sequence of events of this unusual day had really happened. Her corkscrew curls had long ago uncorked. The limp remains were swept up into a ponytail, secured by a shoelace Mrs. Calabria had provided.

Shay closed her eyes and took a deep breath. The breeze was heavenly—sweet and cool on her sweaty face. She glanced back at Sonny, reclining against a corner wall of the crumbling stone villa, one long leg propped on the waist-high railing he was seated upon, the other planted on the cracked pink bricks. This time he smiled more fully. Shay thought it was a beautiful smile.

"We did it, Garrett," Shay said, and pumped her fist to the sky. "Yesss!"

"We're the dynamic duo. Now come over here and share the view."

Shay self-consciously looked down at her feet. She could only imagine what she must look like. She had carefully avoided any and all mirrors she happened across, but she could see her mud-splattered boots and jeans, the T-shirt that had been soaked through with a combination of sweat and rain so many times she doubted it could be salvaged. And that wasn't Opium perfume she smelled! "Maybe I should freshen up first."

Sonny threw back his head and laughed. "Ah, vanity, thy name is woman."

Shay gave him a level gaze. "You're the one who had all the hang-ups about looks, Garrett," she said, and it came out the way she wanted—easy and ironic and amused—but inside Mary Jane's heart pounded.

Sonny was looking at her in a way that was both thoughtful and intense. "We need to talk, Shay. That is, I need to talk and you need to listen. Come here."

"Why?"

"Just come here. Please."

She did. He pulled her down to the railing. Shay was too tired to resist—wasn't sure she wanted to resist.

"Take a deep breath and relax."

She did that too. She leaned back against him, her

head comfortably resting on his broad shoulder, his arms enfolding her, his chin settled on her head.

Well-entrenched ivy ran along the railing and climbed up the walls of the villa. A tangle of wild roses, still heavy with rain, tumbled out to dripping trees outlined against a calm, star-laden sky. A brilliant white crescent moon hung in it. Obadiah raced in muddy circles while Bruno and Dryfuss sniffed around a tree that Corfu had just effortlessly scaled. The lights of a city were on the crest of a hill in silhouette, small against the vast sky.

"Reggio says that's Lucca," Shay said. "We aren't in the middle of nowhere, after all."

"And we weren't lost," Sonny submitted.

"Oh, we were lost all right, Garrett, and we might have been eaten alive by bears."

"I don't think bears are native to Italy."

"Okay, wolves. And they've probably already sent out a search party to find our bones. That was supposed to be a ninety-minute drive, tops."

"Good luck finding us here. Besides, I don't think anybody's going anywhere on the roads around here tonight."

"Reggio said he'd take us to Lucca first thing in the morning," Shay said. "We'll let everyone know we're still alive, and then I'm going to soak in a bubble bath until I'm pruny. Maybe I'll even look halfway human again by the time we have to go onstage at seven-thirty. Riace insists that Samilee and Junior stay here for a few days, until Samilee is up to traveling. That's by Mrs. Calabria's standards, not Samilee's. Riace says there's a good doctor in Lucca that her husband can bring back with him to check Samilee and Junior over, just to be on the safe side. And—''

''You're babbling again, and you're supposed to be listening,'' Sonny reminded her. ''There are a few things I have to get off my chest.''

''Such as?''

''For starters, the conversation you overheard that day at The Donut Shop. J. T. filled me in while we were waiting for you and Samilee at the pizzeria.''

''He shouldn't have done that,'' Shay said, and shrugged out of Sonny's embrace.

She managed to put only a short distance between them before wilting against the onslaught of memories, gazing out at the canine corps and their new best friend. Corfu had come down from the tree and was leisurely bathing himself while the dogs looked on with rapt attention.

''I'm glad he did,'' Sonny said. ''I did you an injustice that I may never be able to make up for.'' He came up behind her, then gently nudged her around so that they were facing each other. ''I honestly didn't remember that, Mary Jane.''

''Don't call me that! Mary Jane ceased to exist a long time ago.''

''I'm sorry to hear that. She was a beautiful person. I was just too blind to see it.''

"Oh, please," Shay said, dragging the six-letter word into several syllables. "I was pathetic. A nerd, or geek, whatever you and your cool crowd called people like me back then. And I was a porker."

"You were beautiful inside. I was a jerk."

Shay looked down for a moment, her lips trembling; then she looked back up at Sonny. "Yes, you definitely were a jerk, and that doesn't even begin to cover it. But that's ancient history, Sonny, and I suppose I should be thanking you."

Sonny shook his head in confusion. "Now you've totally lost me."

Shay's head dropped a few inches as she studied the cracked pink bricks; then she told Sonny how he had contributed to the development of Shay Benton and her career.

"Well?" she asked when the beat of silence lengthened. "Aren't you going to say something?"

Sonny's mouth opened, closed, opened, closed, like a wooden dummy manipulated by a ventriloquist with laryngitis. Finally, he chuckled softly and said, "I really don't know what to say. 'I'm sorry' just doesn't seem to cut it. I can't believe I was so stupid. My mama raised me better than that, and I'd hate to think what she'd have to say about this if she knew what I put you through." But his impassioned words were silenced as Shay pulled his head down, finding his lips with her own.

"You're babbling, Garrett," she said quietly.

He cupped her face in his hands, kissing the tip of her nose. "I adore you, Shay Benton."

Shay raised her head in defiance. "I'm still partly Mary Jane, and always will be."

"I know that. If I hadn't been so full of myself when I first met you I would have known that you were something special. I think I knew it, in my heart. Unfortunately, my eyes did the judging."

"And I wasn't Tammy Sue Brenneman." Shay could hear the sarcastic edge rising in her voice. She didn't like it, but she couldn't stop it.

"You're jealous," Sonny said, encircling her waist with his hands and pulling her closer.

"Am not."

"Are too."

"Am not," Shay said. Then, as Sonny dipped his head, they shared a long and lingering kiss.

"I have an extra ticket to the football game Saturday night," Sonny murmured against her ear. "Know anybody who might be interested in using it?"

Shay nibbled on his earlobe. "I'm sure J. T. would love to go to the game, but we'll be in Rome on Saturday."

Sonny took a step backward. "Rome?" he asked, as if questioning what he'd just heard. "When am I going to see you again?"

"Are you asking me that question, or are you asking the person you met on a beach in Greece? The one who didn't look half bad in a bikini."

"I'm not going to deny that you were pretty easy on the eyes in that bikini. But it's not a figure or a face I fell in love with. If it was, I sure wouldn't be saying those words to you now, lady, because, I hate to tell you this, but you look like a drowned rat."

"You sweet-talker."

"Boy, are you going to be trouble." He yanked on her ponytail. She wrinkled her nose at him, then smiled. He brushed his lips over her half-open mouth. "I know you don't need taking care of, and I know such sentiments are out of fashion in this day and age, but I'm a big, strong guy, and I sure would like to take care of you, ma'am. Do you think you might be able to work a wedding into your schedule sometime soon?"

This time Shay was the one with laryngitis. Her eyes welled up.

"Well, aren't you going to say something—anything?" Sonny asked.

And there was something so husbandly in his tone that Shay laughed and shouted, "Yes!"

"You will?" Sonny's look of pleased surprise was followed by one of such blazing joy that Shay felt her throat tighten.

He pulled her to him. The sweetness of his kiss flowed through her, washing away all of Mary Jane's heartbreak. Then Sonny pointed to the sky. "See there!"

Shay looked but didn't see what he had pointed to

until he pressed his warm hands to the sides of her face and tilted it toward the right quadrant of the sky. Then she did see it: a shooting star scratching its fire across the inky blue.

"I've got what I wished for," she said.

He kissed her forehead. "Me too."

The canine corps, lined up with Tuna Breath on the edge of the veranda, barked. Bruno, then Dryfuss, and finally Obadiah, as if they understood what had been said, and approved.